Savannah tried not to look

But Matt was a magnet. The gray T-shirt clinging to his back was nearly black with sweat. His dark brown hair was wet and thick against his strong neck. Through her open window it seemed the wind carried his scent to her.

The urge to close her eyes and inhale, to stick out her tongue just a little bit and taste the air that had touched him, was nearly stronger than her. For so long she'd been in control of these sudden cravings. And now they threatened to take over.

Which added a spice to Matt that was infinitely appealing. At least to Savannah.

This was worse than inappropriate. These ridiculous feelings she had for him were flat-out wrong. Wrong because he worked for her and wrong because he was a stranger and wrong because...well, just wrong.

Dear Reader,

I have wished, more times than I can count, that I was Southern. Not just so I could have an heirloom pecan pie recipe, though that would be fantastic. And not just so I could say "bless your heart" and have it mean the many nice and not so nice things it seems to mean when Southern women say it. But so I could have serious skeletons in my closet. And I could walk around in a slip like Elizabeth Taylor in *Cat on a Hot Tin Roof* and not catch pneumonia.

But I am not Southern. I am from the Midwest and I moved to Canada. But my Deep South fantasies are now being played out on the page in this very fun new series—THE NOTORIOUS O'NEILLS—about a Louisiana family plagued by family secrets, stolen gems and broken hearts.

I am often asked what inspires me about a certain idea, and I usually say something lame, such as love is always inspiring. But here is the truth: I love the heroes. I love torturing them, redeeming them; I love taking their shirts off. Heroes are why I adore romance novels. As I started Savannah's book, I swore this book was going to be about her. And how could it not? A betrayed woman, locked up in a prison of her own making, she was a heroine I could sink my teeth into. But then onto the page walked Matt Woods. And I was totally intrigued by the question, what makes a good guy go bad?

I hope you enjoy the first book in this series. Please drop me a line at www.molly-okeefe.com. I love to hear from readers!

Happy reading,

Molly O'Keefe

The Temptation of Savannah O'Neill
Molly O'Keefe

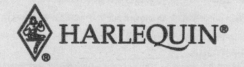

HARLEQUIN®

TORONTO • NEW YORK • LONDON
AMSTERDAM • PARIS • SYDNEY • HAMBURG
STOCKHOLM • ATHENS • TOKYO • MILAN • MADRID
PRAGUE • WARSAW • BUDAPEST • AUCKLAND

Recycling programs
for this product may
not exist in your area.

ISBN-13: 978-0-373-71651-7

THE TEMPTATION OF SAVANNAH O'NEILL

Copyright © 2010 by Molly Fader.

This edition published by arrangement with Harlequin Books S.A.

For questions and comments about the quality of this book
please contact us at Customer_eCare@Harlequin.ca.

www.eHarlequin.com

Printed in U.S.A.

ABOUT THE AUTHOR

In her fantasy life Molly O'Keefe gets pedicures every week while a team of manly maids cleans her house. Dinner gets made every night by someone else and it never includes a meatball or macaroni. She lives on a beach. Oh! In Hawaii. In real life, she's married to a great guy with two lovely children and lives in Toronto, Canada. Where she never finds the time to get pedicures.

Books by Molly O'Keefe

I met my best friend in kindergarten almost thirty years ago. She inspires me every day with her strength, commitment and capacity for junk food. This book is for Allycia.

CHAPTER ONE

"KATIE," SAVANNAH O'Neill sang. "Come out, come out wherever you are."

She snuck up to the mountainous rosebush, searching through the wild abundance of pink tea roses for a glimpse of red curly hair, a freckled cheek or bright blue eyes.

"Gotcha!" she cried, pushing apart the thorny branches only to find C.J., the orange tabby, sleeping beneath its leaves.

No Katie.

This is getting ridiculous, she thought.

A quick Saturday morning game of hide-and-seek with her eight-year-old was beginning to take all day. Savannah pushed through the kudzu vines, ivy and weeping willow branches that dominated the back courtyard, but Katie wasn't in any of her usual spots.

She'd upped her game.

Savannah tripped over a broken cobblestone, catching herself against a thick blanket of kudzu vines that had eaten up the fountain and obliterated the bird feeder.

It was getting very third world back here. Soon enough, these games with Katie would require a machete.

That would add a whole new dimension to kamikaze hide-and-seek.

"I told you," she called out. "You can run but you can't hide."

The branches of the cypress rustled over her head and Savannah smiled, backtracking to the trunk of the old tree.

It was only a matter of time, Savannah thought, before Katie worked up the courage to climb the tree. The hundred-year-old cypress was a beauty—bigger than the two-story house in front of it, and its roots were pushing through the cobblestones, breaking up the courtyard like some kind of underground monster.

As if it had been yesterday, Savannah's foot found the small lee in the trunk, her hands found the knobs on the lower branches and within seconds she was halfway up into the leaves. She was careful to look for snakes, and hoped her daughter had done the same.

What, she wondered, would her clients say if they could see their staid researcher now? The kids at the library, who made faces at her behind her back, would fall over their stolen library books if they saw mean old Ms. O'Neill climbing trees.

Savannah found her daughter lying across one of the thick branches directly over the decrepit greenhouse and back stone wall of the property. The girl had only been up two hours and the new red silk pajamas Margot had brought back from her cruise in the Far East were covered in dirt and leaves.

"Found you!" Savannah cried. "You're doing dishes."

"Shh!" Katie hissed, not turning away from whatever scene she was spying on.

"What's up?" Savannah whispered, climbing a parallel branch, shimmying out over the courtyard on her belly.

"Margot," Katie whispered. Savannah watched her daughter push the red tangle of curls behind her ear, revealing her freckled face, her wide lips and long nose. Not pretty, her little girl—even through her mother's eyes, Savannah could see that. But Katie was so much more than pretty. She was tough. Independent. Beautiful in her own wild way. Pure at heart.

Everything, Savannah thought, *I am not.*

"I think she's crying," Katie said.

Savannah tore her eyes from her daughter and sought out Margot's thin and elegant form amongst the weeds and broken buildings beneath them.

"Back wall," Katie said. "Someone wrote something on the stones."

Not again, Savannah thought. She saw Margot, wearing her white linen, pumps and no doubt "the" diamonds scrubbing at the back wall. The letters—*O'NEILL SLU*—

"I can hear you girls up there!" Margot yelled without turning around.

"What are you doing, Margot?" Savannah called.

"Contemplating bear traps," she said and threw the thick yellow sponge into the bucket of water at her feet. Margot turned and faced Savannah in the heat of the morning. Her long white hair was perfect, her face as stunning as the diamonds at her wrists and ears. You would never guess she was pushing eighty.

But right now Margot was one pissed-off matriarch. And when Margot got mad, things got organized. And cleaned. And worst of all, changed.

Savannah's heart leaped into her throat.

Change was the devil. Change had to be avoided at all costs.

Savannah went into instant damage-control mode.

"Every year," Savannah yelled, shimmying back down the tree, shamed by her grandmother's elegance into at least *acting* like an adult. "You know this happens every year. As soon as school gets out for summer, we get every teenager trying to prove to their friends how cool they are."

Why vandalizing their home was considered cool was one of the great mysteries of local teenage life.

She swung down from the lowest branch and landed on the broken cobblestone. Looking up she found Katie carefully scrambling down after her.

"Careful," Savannah said. When Katie got within reach Savannah lifted her daughter down, holding her close for just a second, smelling the sunshine and rose smell of her skin.

The pajamas were toast.

"What does that mean?" Katie asked, pointing to the letters on the stone walls. Savannah shot Margot an arch look—slut was a stretch, but Margot was the closest thing they had.

"Like you have no secrets?" Margot asked, defensive.

"Officially, I'm not an O'Neill."

"Honey, an O'Neill by any other name is still an O'Neill."

The truth was, every O'Neill female was born with secrets, and through their own legendarily bad decision-making, each of them had her own sins. Not that the men had it any better—her brothers had their own crimes and mysteries.

Secrets upon secrets, that was the O'Neill legacy.

And, she had to believe, even if her mother had taken Richard Bonavie's name, the curse would have lingered.

"What does it mean?" Katie asked again.

"It's just a bad word," Savannah said. "Kids think it's funny to write bad words on our back wall."

O'Neill Sluts.

O'Neill Devils.

O'Neill Thieves.

"Was this here while I was gone?" Margot asked, having gotten back a week and half ago from her cruise.

"No!" Savannah denied, though she wasn't totally sure. She loved her jungle, wild and unmaintained, but it obstructed her view of much of the yard. "It's new."

"It'd never been this bad before," Margot said. "Come look at this."

Katie and Savannah headed around the tree and through the kudzu to the greenhouse and back wall. Now that Savannah was closer she saw that Margot was actually very upset. Her fine elegant hands were shaking.

"Look," Margot whispered, pointing to the greenhouse.

Every pane of glass had been shattered and all of Margot's orchids were destroyed. The unearthed roots like veins, strewn across tabletops and the floor. Dirt like blood, everywhere.

"Oh, my lord, Margot." She raised astonished eyes to her grandmother. Occasionally the woman went to New Orleans and played poker, or took a cruise with an "admirer" and gambled across the seven seas, and she used to keep her winnings back here buried in pots because she didn't trust banks. She'd done it for years before Savannah found out and made her stop. "Are you hiding money back here again?"

"No." Margot pulled a face. "I lost on this last one, I told you that."

"Then why would anyone do this?"

"Because it was here. I don't know." She looked around the wreckage, her face drawn. "I understand you hate the idea. But I think it's time."

"No." God, no. Anything but what Margot was suggesting. "Margot, we can do something." Savannah leaned down and started cleaning up, picking up shattered pottery, knowing she was too late—the courtyard was out of control. The boldest of the high school students were drinking back here, and Katie was almost always getting cuts and bruises from the roses and broken cobblestones.

These plants, the trees, the bushes—nothing had been touched in years. Nearly twenty. She knew something should be done, but it was hers. The idea of someone else, some stranger back here, was unthinkable.

Because if they were in her courtyard then they'd be in her home. In her life. And no good ever came of that—pain was an excellent teacher.

"I'll clean it up," Savannah said, feeling a bubble of frantic energy rising in her throat. "I start vacation on Tuesday. I can work on it then."

"I'll help," Katie chimed in, crouching next to her to help and Savannah winked at her, grateful.

"Honey," Margot said, shaking her head. "We both know you're taking the time off to work on that research for the Discovery Channel. There aren't enough hours in the day."

"I'll work at night. Anything, Margot—"

"You've been saying that for years, and it's not just cleaning up the plants anymore. We need the greenhouse rebuilt, the wall needs to be fixed and I think we need an alarm system."

"In our garden?"

Margot flung out a hand to the shattered remains of her greenhouse, the orchids like dead animals. All the evidence she needed, really, to prove that things were getting dangerous.

"Now the greenhouse, next the house?"

Savannah couldn't stand the thought. She looked down at Katie, the messy rumpled perfection of her. Strangers in her garden? Bent on helping? Or, worse, strangers in her house? Bent on mischief? Where her daughter slept?

When put that way, it was an easy call.

"Margot," Savannah sighed. "I'm so sorry."

"They're all gone," Margot said, stepping over glass and flower carnage. "They've ruined everything."

"I'll call Juliette—"

"I already did," Margot said. "She's the one who told me to get someone in here to set up a security system. The police force is too small to have someone watching this house all the time."

Savannah looked around, chagrined and regretful that she'd let things get this bad. She should have done the basic maintenance that would have at least kept things safe. She had, after all, managed to keep the middle courtyard groomed and lovely. A pastoral paradise.

But the back courtyard was hers—it had been from the moment her mother had dropped Savannah and her brothers off with Margot and left without a word. And the truth was, she liked the wilderness of it, the overgrown vines and crumbling statues. The stone walls covered in hens and chicks, the roses pink and red like hidden gems, small beating hearts in a giant breathing body of green.

The air was different back here, too. Thick and fragrant with mystery and magnolias.

Oh, please, she thought, realizing she was on the verge of getting maudlin and depressing. It's a garden. *You are a grown woman who should have more important things to do than get attached to kudzu and rosebushes.*

Or maybe she should have more in her life than kudzu and rosebushes. The thought flickered to life briefly before Savannah extinguished it.

"I know," Margot said, watching Savannah carefully. "We've been alone in this house for so long it seems strange to bring someone else in."

"We don't need anyone else!" Katie cried and Savannah tucked an arm around her daughter, realizing that maybe there was such a thing as too much family unity—considering her eight-year-old was showing signs of xenophobia.

"Margot's right." Savannah sighed and Margot's perfect eyebrows arched slightly in surprise. Savannah ignored the slick twist of distaste in her belly as the words got clogged in her throat. What if someone tried to break into the house? She looked at her daughter, fear crawling over her like ants. "It's time to bring someone else in to take care of this garden."

MATT WOODS STARED at the two-story plantation-style house then down at the surveillance photos in his hand.

He was hunting for Vanessa O'Neill, last seen in New Orleans.

But it was the picture of Vanessa's daughter, Savannah, he couldn't look away from. Glittering and golden, she smiled up at him from her photo.

How much did she know? he wondered. *How guilty was she?*

He scoffed at his own question. Everyone was guilty. No one's hands were clean.

Was she guilty of theft and betrayal like her mother? Or just guilty of bad blood?

Matt rubbed gritty eyes. He'd driven through the night from St. Louis to Bonne Terre, Louisiana, and in the clear light of morning he realized his plan pretty much sucked.

Vanessa had been last seen two weeks ago in New Orleans. Matt knew this because he'd hired an investigator to track down everyone related to the jewel theft that his father had been involved in seven years ago.

His investigator had taken her picture, followed her around to various poker games and bars, and heard her talking about Bonne Terre and the Manor. Then she'd vanished. Just vanished.

Matt connected the dots and decided to come here to find her. Or wait for her. Whatever it took to correct justice's aim.

It's not like he had anything else to do.

So, his plan, if you could call it that, was to see if Vanessa was here. And if she wasn't, he was going to find a reason to wait until she showed up. Or better yet, find out where she was.

"Yeah," he muttered to Savannah's photo. "Not my best work."

Six months ago his life was torn apart, and now he was talking to photos as if they might reply and stalking the O'Neill women to seek retribution for a seven-year-old crime.

"Justice," he said to the photo, tasting the word, loving how it gave him a purpose. A fire.

But not a plan.

"What am I supposed to do with you?" he asked the photo.

He could knock on the door and…what? He considered Savannah's smile, the radiance that poured from her eyes. She was like sun off of glass, she just seemed to shimmer.

Was he going to threaten her? Interrogate her? Tie her up while he waited for her mother to arrive? And then hope that the mother just happened to be traveling with a fortune in stolen gems?

Had he come to that? Really?

"Great, Woods," Matt said, rubbing his hands over his face. "Sherlock Holmes, you are not."

Suddenly, he had a memory of sitting outside an Indian reservation casino. He must have been about eight or nine, and his father was going in for one quick game. One hand. Just one.

He told Matt that his job was to sit in the car and watch for three men. One man with a patch, another with a scar and the final man with a one of those Russian bearskin hats. When Matt saw those three men he needed to run inside the casino and find Joel.

Clever, Matt realized now, twenty-five years later. Because while men with scars and patches were a possibility in South Carolina, there would be no bearskin hats.

A goose chase. A fool's errand, his father was brilliant with them. A master. And Matt had taken his job so seriously he'd sat in that beat-up Chevy with a notebook and pen, drawing pictures and taking notes, a young Sherlock Holmes. Always keen. Always on the lookout for a bearskin hat that would never come.

All of which was irrelevant. Every moment of the past, every bad decision and terrible accident that led him to this point, was moot.

The only thing that mattered now was making one thing right, in a life gone horribly wrong. He had to make one damn thing right. Who betrayed Dad? Joel's partner, Richard Bonavie, or the blonde at the drop-off—Vanessa O'Neill?

The legal system might have gotten it wrong with Matt, whose hands were bloody right down to the bone, but it wasn't too late to get justice for his father. That's why he was here, and the women inside that house were the key to it all.

He angled the rearview mirror and checked his reflection—a little closer to potential ax murderer than was entirely necessary, but there wasn't much he could do. He forgot a razor.

The scruff of his beard rasped under his hands and he

thought about all his clients, hiring the cool and slick Matt Woods to design their summer homes, their art galleries and condos.

That guy doesn't live here anymore, he thought, unable to recognize himself in the green eyes that stared back.

Matt threw open the door of his rented car and slammed it behind him. What he lacked in plans he was going to make up for in bravado. Some righteous "where the hell is your mother?"

Smooth. Oh, so smooth.

The bayou around him seemed to pulse and breathe. It was warmer than St. Louis, denser, the air thick and somehow both sweet and spicy. Like flowers dipped in cayenne.

He liked it. It made him hungry for food and a woman at the same time.

The house, he assessed with an knowledgeable eye, was an aging stunner. It sat alone on the road, about a mile and a half from town, surrounded by a few acres of wilderness. She was a grand dame falling on hard times—the black trim was peeling and a few of the white hurricane shutters were missing slats. But the bones of the house were solid. Elegant. Built to withstand the Southern weather, and to look good doing it.

He imagined the windows lit with candles and the sound of music and ice in crystal tumblers spilling from the open front door.

The front door was freshly, brazenly painted scarlet.

Matt believed doors could be sexy. He believed windows and wood and concrete could be erotic. But nothing he'd ever seen quite matched the sexual statement of that red door.

It looked like the house of an aging mistress, an expensive woman of slightly ill repute, which would be Margot's influence. But he didn't know how Savannah the librarian fit in.

He stepped up the river-stone path, the rocks sliding under his old work boots. He'd packed work clothes, denim and rawhide, because the expensive suits, silk ties and Italian leather in his closet were beginning to mock him.

He got one foot onto the wide steps of the sweeping veranda and the scarlet door creaked open.

Margot O'Neill, he knew from the surveillance photo in the car. She stood in the doorway, the black of the hall behind her making her fair beauty more pronounced. More breathtaking, despite her years.

She was medium height and trim, with posture like a steel beam. She wore bright blue and the fabric looked rich and thin—like liquid had been poured over her.

It was no wonder men paid to have her. She was that beautiful. That rare.

And then she smiled, like she knew it.

"You're coming about the ad?" she asked, her voice rich with years of the South.

Ad? Damn not having a plan. She tilted her head, her blue eyes losing some of their hospitality, and he knew he was moments from being kicked off the property.

"Yes," he finally said, taking yet another leap into the unknown. "I am. I'm here about the ad."

Good God, he hoped he wasn't about to be Margot's boy toy. Though there *could* be worse things, he speculated, catching the gleam in her eye.

"Margot, are you—" The door opened farther and a blonde goddess stood in the dark hallway. Matt's heart stopped dead in his chest.

It was Savannah, from the photograph.

Sort of.

The beauty was there, the perfect skin, bright blue eyes

and shiny sweep of hair. But that was where the similarities ended. The real-life Savannah was somehow sharper, her radiance hard and refined to an edge. Her cheekbones alone could cut through tin.

She was razor wire next to Margot's magnolia.

There was no sunny warmth. No shimmer. This woman was a stranger to him. He knew this was ridiculous—picture or no, she was still a stranger to him. But the loss was there nonetheless. He didn't realize how much he was looking forward to basking in that warm glow—until that glow was buried under ice.

She was, however, painfully sexy in a long straight gray skirt and a white shirt that couldn't quite diminish the curves she clearly was trying to hide. The whole look gave her the appearance of a prison warden on lockdown.

In a porno.

And, he realized, aside from sexy she was also a dead ringer for the surveillance picture he had of Vanessa in New Orleans. Right down to the eyes, which were guarded. Wary. Hiding something.

He lost his companion, that fantasy woman, but he gained something else. Something better. Something righteous.

In a stunning moment of clarity, he knew that coming here, believing these women somehow had the answers he needed, had not been wrong.

It occurred to him that the missing gems, the Pacific Diamond and Ruby—the million-dollar reasons his father sat alone in a jail cell while his accomplices and turncoats lived in freedom—could be right here.

Hidden and guarded by Savannah O'Neill.

Out of the corner of his eye he took in the crumbling house, the faded paint, the sagging porch. That the gems were here now, or ever had been, seemed like a long shot.

"Oh, sorry," she said, looking at Matt with plain distaste. "Who are you?"

"He's here about the ad," Margot said, standing aside and smiling at Matt. "Please come in."

His lip curled, satisfaction rippling through him. Savannah must have sensed it, because her own lips tightened, her eyes narrowed.

He hitched the loose waist of his worn khakis and climbed the steps, feeling the heat of the South mesh with the sudden warmth in his flesh. His eyes stayed glued to Savannah's as something primal swept through him.

You, he thought, *have a secret. And I will find out what it is.*

CHAPTER TWO

"MARGOT," SAVANNAH MUTTERED as the strange man climbed the stairs, like some kind of predatory cat, all muscle and intention. His shaggy brown hair gleamed like polished wood and his green eyes radiated something hot and awful that she felt in the core of her body—a trembling where there hadn't been one in years. Hot sweat ran between her breasts under her white cotton shirt. "This is not a good idea."

"Please, Savannah," Margot all but purred, her eyes hovering over the man like a honeybee. "Look at him. It's a fabulous idea."

Savannah's hand tightened on the door as if her muscles were about to override her system and slam the door in his handsome, chiseled face.

But then he was there, big and masculine on the tattered welcome mat. C.J., the little tart, stepped out of the sleeping porch to curl around his dusty boots.

Seriously, that cat gave all of them a bad name.

"My name is Matt Howe," he said, holding out his hand.

Margot shook it, clasping Matt's big paw in her lily-white one. "I'm Margot O'Neill," she said. "Welcome to my home."

Then it was Savannah's turn.

Her turn to touch his flesh to hers. Her turn to stand under his neon gaze.

Just a man, she told herself. *Tell yourself he's a client. He wants research on minor battles in the Pacific during World War Two or about the migratory patterns of long-tailed swallows.*

Her hand slid into his and receptors, long buried, long ignored, shook themselves awake, sighing with a sudden pleasure.

"Savannah O'Neill," she said, her voice a brusque rattle.

"A pleasure, Savannah," Matt said, bowing slightly over her hand.

Pretend, she told herself, yanking her hand free from his callused, strong grip, *that he's gay.*

But the way his eyes climbed quickly over her body belied that particular fantasy.

Pretend you *are gay,* she told herself. But the heat in her belly ruined her pretense.

"Your ad was a little vague," he said, stammering slightly on the words. "I was hoping for some more information about what you're looking for?"

Savannah cast a quick, dubious look at Margot. What about *Handyman/gardener needed* was vague? Despite the sharpness in his eyes, the guy clearly wasn't all that bright.

"Margot," she said, grabbing her grandmother's elbow. "Perhaps we—"

"Should show him the courtyard," Margot said, smiling at Matt and shaking off Savannah's hand. "So he can see the scope of the work."

Margot was determined—more determined now that a man was here, handsome and virile, stepping into the Manor—than she'd been in front of the greenhouse two days ago, cradling her dead orchids.

Savannah began to sense that this was wrong in more ways than they could possibly fathom.

Men in general were a danger to the O'Neill women; it had been proven time and time again men brought out the worst in them. The most notorious aspects of their already inappropriate characters.

Even her.

Especially her.

But handsome strangers? They were catnip to a certain kind of woman—and Margot was one of those women.

Right, she nearly laughed aloud at her own blindness, *and you're so immune.*

It had been years since her heart had thundered in her chest like this—and that had not ended all that well.

"I've lived in this house my whole life," Margot was saying, her hand cradled in Matt's elbow as she led them through the shabby manor as if it was still the best property in the area. "And my mother did the same before me."

"It's a beautiful house," Matt said, glancing up at the high ceilings, all of which needed spackle and paint. The mahogany floors beneath their feet were beginning to buckle and sag in places and she watched as Margot led him around the worst patches, as though they were avoiding puddles in the rain. "Did your family build it?" He asked.

Savannah laughed and Margot tossed her a wicked look over her shoulder. "Yes," Margot said. "My great-great-grandfather built this house."

As a saloon and whorehouse.

She noticed Margot wasn't advertising that fact.

The devil in Savannah wanted to point out the origins of the house, just to watch Margot's skin get splotchy and Matt get flustered, but Savannah spent so much time pretending not to be born from a long line of gamblers and whores that she couldn't bring herself to say it.

No matter its comedic value.

They stepped from the dark hall, with its offshoots of parlor, dining room and library, through the glass doors into the middle courtyard.

"Beautiful," Matt said, and Savannah wondered if he really meant it. He seemed to. All that predatory intensity was dialed down for a moment as his eyes swept over the hedges and lilies she kept in order.

"Yes," Margot agreed, with a sideways look at Savannah. "The middle courtyard is not the problem."

The phone rang inside the house and Margot cast Savannah a pleading look, which Savannah scowled at.

Right. She was going to leave this strange man alone with her aging grandmother. Particularly when said aging grandmother insisted on wearing the only real jewelry they had left that was worth anything. The diamonds that were, according to Margot, a thank-you gift from a certain president of Irish heritage. *Please.*

"I'll be right back," Margot said, giving Matt's arm a squeeze. "My granddaughter will show you the rest of the way."

Margot left, blue silk fluttering behind her.

"Grandmother?" he said. "She looks like she could be your mother."

"She's not," Savannah said. The subject of daughters and mothers was not discussed at the Manor. And fathers? Well, it simply never came up.

"Is your mother here?" he asked, and Savannah stared hard at Matt, as if to see past his green eyes and strong arms to the heart beating under that lean chest.

He stared right back at her, his eyes wide open as if he had nothing to hide.

Of course, that had to be a lie. Everyone had something to hide. Everyone.

"No," she said. "She isn't. I'll show you the back courtyard."

She led him through a second set of glass doors into a brighter hall leading left to the kitchens and cellars and right to the upstairs bedrooms.

"So why don't you call her grandmother?" Matt asked and Savannah rolled her eyes.

"Does she look like a grandmother?"

Matt smiled. "Good point. Does anyone else live here?"

Her eyes bored right through him. "That doesn't have anything to do with our garden," she said.

"Yes, but—"

She pushed open the old oak doors to the bright sunlight and overgrown majesty of her secret garden.

"Holy—" he breathed, stepping up beside her.

"The greenhouse needs to be repaired, and the trees, bushes, flowers and weeds all need to be dealt with." She pointed to the worst of them, along the west wall. "There—" she indicated the center cluster of kudzu under the cypress "—is a bird feeder and bench under that mess that we'd like to see again. The back wall—" she swept her arm over to where the graffiti had been cleaned "—needs to be fixed and we think we need some security cameras—"

"Security? Why?"

"High school students like to break in, cause some trouble." She shrugged, trying to be nonchalant. But she could tell he was reading the words they couldn't quite get off the back wall.

Her whole body burned with embarrassment.

"High school students did that?" he asked, pointing to

the wrecked greenhouse, and she nodded. "Seems like a matter for the police."

"We've tried that," she said. And that was all she said. She wasn't giving this man more than what he absolutely needed.

His eyes scanned the property as if he were putting price tags on everything.

And she didn't like that one bit.

He was probably wondering what could be stolen, despite the tour he'd had through the shabby manor, stripped of its antique furniture and silver. Those diamonds Margot sported and Savannah's own small fortune in computer equipment were the only things of value left. But Matt didn't know that.

"Looks like a reasonable job," Matt said, staring at the mess. "I'll take it."

Incredulous, she swiveled on her heel to gape at him. "Really?" she asked, crossing her arms over her chest. "Don't you want to know more about the money? The living situation?"

His cheeks turned red and he nodded. "Of course."

"First," she said. "I have a few questions of my own."

"Fire away." He held his arms out the sides, his gray T-shirt hugging the lean muscles in his stomach.

"Where are you from?"

"St. Louis. I've been…working with an architecture firm there for the last few years."

"What are you doing here?" she asked, trying to ignore a bead of sweat trickling down the side of Matt's strong, bronzed neck.

"I heard there was a lot of work in Louisiana."

She couldn't argue with that—it seemed the state needed to be rebuilt top to bottom.

"You're, what? Thirtysomething?"

"Thirty-four."

"And you can just up and leave St. Louis? You have no responsibilities?"

"None that won't keep for a while."

"Are you on the run?"

"From the law?" His lip curled as if he was laughing at her and her head snapped back at the insult. The man had no reason to laugh. Not here, not now. He quickly shook his head, his smile gone. "I'm not running from the law."

"My best friend is police chief in town, she can find out if you're lying."

"She's welcome to," he said, his dark eyes guileless. "I haven't broken any laws."

"A woman? A family? Have you left behind some kids?" She nearly spat the words.

"No," he said quickly, sounding horrified. "No, of course not. I know you don't know me, but I wouldn't do that."

She had no reason to trust him, but in this area she did. For some reason the earnest horror in his eyes seemed sincere.

He wouldn't leave behind kids.

She had to give him some points for that.

"Do you have some references?"

"References?"

"Yes," she said. "I believe it's standard to offer some proof of your reliability before I give you carte blanche with my garden."

He laughed. "It's hardly a garden—"

"References," she said, not about to listen to him disparage her refuge. She pulled her cell phone free from her shirt pocket. "Let's start with that architecture firm in St. Louis."

Perhaps it was a trick of the sun, but Matt seemed to go white.

A PLAN WOULD HAVE BEEN good. Something concrete. Something that wasn't going to get him arrested, because Savannah was staring at him as though she would like nothing better than to send his sorry butt right to the nearest jail cell.

Prison warden wasn't even the half of it. Savannah O'Neill was judge, jury and executioner.

"Steel and Wood Architecture," he managed to say and then, because all she did was arch an eyebrow, he gave her the number. The direct number to his office.

This is never, ever going to work.

Erica, his assistant, was a wizard, but this might prove to be too much. What were the odds that she would remember Howe was his mother's maiden name?

He watched Savannah from the corner of his eye while pretending to assess the broken cobblestones of the steps they stood on.

"Hi. Erica, is it?" she said into her cell phone and Matt stooped to inspect the ivy overtaking the stones. He touched a gray-green leaf with shaking fingers. "My name is Savannah O'Neill. I'm considering hiring a Matt Howe to do some gardening and repair work around my home and he gave me Steel and Wood Architecture as a reference…Matt Howe. Howe." She tilted the phone away from her mouth and Matt felt like his head might pop off from the blood pressure building in his neck. "Is that with an *e* at the end?" she asked.

He nodded, stupidly.

Seriously, Woods. You're a self-made millionaire, you were on the cover of—

"He did?" Savannah asked, sounding skeptical. "He was?" That didn't sound much better. Matt wondered what kind of explanation was going to be needed when she called the cops. A cash explanation? "Best employee the firm ever had?"

He swiveled to face Savannah who stared at him, revealing nothing. He shrugged, as if being the model employee was something that came naturally.

She smiled slightly, almost bashfully, the sunshine cutting through her hair and illuminating her skin, making it shimmer.

Matt felt like he'd been sucker punched. *This* was the woman from the surveillance photo, the woman he'd been talking to. She did live somewhere inside that cold shell.

Something pulled and tightened in his chest. A recognition where there hadn't been one before.

Her sharp edges seemed softened, blurred somehow as she stood there, sunshine glittering around her. She was Ingrid Bergman, vulnerable and stoic and so beautiful it hurt to look at her.

The fact that he wanted to drown himself in her, the way he had in scotch immediately after the accident, was a bad omen.

It was better that he not recognize her. Better that he not like her. Not care about her. He'd committed himself to this ruse, and liking her would only cloud the waters.

"Yes," she finally said, still on the phone with Erica, who would be getting a huge raise. "Thank you, Erica. Here he is." Savannah handed her cell to Matt. "She wants to talk to you."

I'll bet she does.

He took the phone as if it were a snake, coiled to strike, and stepped down the broken stone steps for some privacy.

"Thank you, Erica," he murmured.

"Oh, you'd *better* thank me, Matt!" Erica cried and he

winced at the daggers in her tone. "Where the hell have you been?"

"I—"

"You know, a better question is what the hell are you doing? Applying for some job as a gardener, are you nuts?"

Yes. Slightly.

"No, Erica, I'm just…" What? Doing some reconnaissance? A little private investigative work? "Getting some R and R. That's all."

"For six months?"

Six months, two weeks, and three days. "Who's counting," he said.

"I am!" she nearly screamed. "Your clients are. While you're getting some R and R," she spat the words as if they were sour, "I'm trying to keep the bills paid and the money coming in. Your clients, you remember them, don't you? The people who pay you huge amounts of money to build stuff? Well, most of them are getting antsy and Joe Collins is about to sue for breach of—"

Matt hung up.

It was so simple. He hit the red button with his thumb and his life, that kid, his best friend and partner, his job, the buildings he could no longer build, they went away.

Gone.

Instead there was the whirr and snick of cicadas hiding in leaves so dense, so green they looked black. An orange cat curled around his boots and the sun beat down on his head.

Numb. So numb to all that used to be.

Savannah stood behind him. He could feel her like a shadow over his face on a hot day. A mystery. A cool-eyed, blond-haired mystery.

That was it. That was all his world consisted of right now.

Because outside of this, this moment, this place, this

mysterious woman, a point-seven-second nightmare waited for him, pacing the perimeter for the chance to attack.

Point-seven seconds was all it took for a building to come down. For a mistake to be made and a young man to die. Point-seven seconds. It was enough to make a guy go crazy if he thought about it long enough.

And Matt had been thinking about it for six months, two weeks and three days.

"Well," Savannah said. "It sounds like Margot and I are lucky you were wandering through."

"Do I have the job?" he asked, his voice rough even to his own ears.

He felt her at his shoulder and he turned, surprised to see her so close. She had a spray of freckles across her nose. And her eyes weren't totally blue. They were like the Caribbean before a storm—blue and turquoise with gray shadows rolling underneath.

"Yes," she said and stepped closer. Close enough that he could smell her skin, flowers and sweat, so earthy and feminine it immediately conjured thoughts of her naked on silk sheets. "But you stay out of our house. You stay out of our business. There's a hotel in town. You can stay there. You arrive at eight and you leave at five. You can use the bathroom on the main floor and that's it. No exceptions."

He rocked back, stunned at the vehemence.

She's hiding something, he thought, knowing it was the truth because he could taste it on her breath.

"Got it?" she asked.

He nodded. "Got it."

"Starting tomorrow, I'm taking a vacation week, so I'll be here."

Keeping an eye on you—she didn't have to say it, and Matt didn't know whether to laugh or be insulted.

She reached up and gathered that long silky fall of hair into a ponytail then she curled it around itself, tucking it and wrapping it until it was all but gone, vanished into a tight knot at the back of her head.

"And do not—" she actually poked him once in the chest with a blunt, naked nail, hard enough to hurt "—mess up my garden."

Then, Savannah O'Neill, sexiest prison warden ever, was gone.

He stood there, dumbfounded by the complex reality of that woman in the photograph.

"I'm going to work!" He heard her yell inside the house and he turned, staring out at the jungle and ruins that made up his new job.

He nearly laughed, stunned at how this had all worked out.

He could wait for Vanessa to show up in her very own backyard.

Not sure of what he should do, he decided he'd wait for Margot to fill him in on the rest of the details. He stepped away from the house toward the ruins of the greenhouse, taking in the damage. It was far more extensive than he'd first seen.

He jostled one of the remaining posts of the structure and some stubborn piece of glass shattered onto the broken cobblestone at his feet.

Someone had gone to town on the building—and the plants that had been growing inside. Parts of it had been cleaned up, but the shards of pottery and dead orchids were piled in the corner.

And there were a lot of dead orchids.

"Working already?" Margot's soft voice snapped him out of his focus and he jerked as if caught doing something he shouldn't.

"I guess so," he lied.

"It's a lot of work, isn't it?" she asked, and something in her tone had him glancing at her and seeing, for a brief moment, past her beauty and the sunshot diamonds to the sadness beneath her glitter. And he didn't want to see that. At all. He didn't want to feel anything besides suspicion for these women.

Well, suspicion and lust for Savannah perhaps. But no sympathy. No empathy.

He forced his attention back to the space he was supposed to salvage. All he saw was damage. Broken glass and twisted metal. A year ago he would have seen endless possibilities, now he saw nothing. Nothing but destruction.

He felt, looking at all this ruin, a certain kinship with the courtyard.

"It's not too bad," he lied.

"This used to be my favorite place," Margot said, her fingers touching the edge of an old worktable that had been smashed.

He bit back a groan. *Don't,* he thought. *Don't open up to the hired help.*

She gestured halfheartedly at the dead plants. "I grew orchids."

"You will again." This lame platitude sounded flat on his tongue, like a lie but different. Worse, somehow. Because she brightened, bought into the false hope he hadn't intended to give.

"I hope so."

"Why would someone do this?" he asked, watching her carefully, pretending to be casual. "Was there something of value in here?"

"In a greenhouse?" Margot asked, sliding him a sideways look.

He couldn't read her private grin, but it made him think

there had been something worth smashing a greenhouse for in those pots.

He shrugged. "Seems like someone went to a lot of trouble over some orchids."

"It's a tradition around here, I'm afraid." She turned gem-bright eyes to him. "The O'Neills are a bit of a target. That's why Savannah can seem a bit—" she shrugged "—cool."

This insight was totally unwelcome. But it explained a lot about the prickly Savannah.

"You mean this sort of destruction happens a lot?" he asked, stunned at the thought.

"It's summer break," Margot said. "High school students get bored in a small town and we've managed to provide enough entertainment to become somewhat... legendary."

"Why don't you leave?"

Margot blinked at him. "This is my home," she said as if he'd suggested she cut off her ear. "How could I leave?"

Why would you stay? he thought. But then, maybe that was his problem. It had been too easy for him to leave everything behind.

"Savannah said I had the job," he said.

Margot's eyes went wide for a second, surprise showing clearly on her face before she carefully erased it. Hid it. Those eyes were bottomless, a place where secrets lived.

These women know something.

"Well, if Savannah says so, it must be true." Margot tipped her head. "Our budget is three thousand dollars, I know it's not much, but you can stay in the sleeping porch—"

Matt laughed.

"What's so funny?"

"I'm pretty sure staying in the sleeping porch was not part of Savannah's plan. She mentioned a hotel in town."

Margot smiled, her eyes canny, and Matt found himself liking the old lady. "It's my home, Matt. You are welcome to stay in the porch."

Right. Like he was going to get caught in the middle of this family squabble. "I'll stay in the hotel tonight," he said. "Let you break the news to her."

"Oh, Matt, I can tell already you are a wise man." She tilted her head, her sapphire eyes studying him. "Then, I guess the only question is, do *you* want the job?"

Matt tried not to smile too confidently. Too broadly. He tried, actually, not to crow with pleasure and satisfaction. "Absolutely."

CHAPTER THREE

EVERYONE THOUGHT libraries were quiet. Savannah never understood that. In all the years she'd spent hiding, studying, teaching and working in libraries, she'd found each and every one of them loud. Filled with sound, actually. Like one of those seashells you pressed to your ear.

There was an endless ocean of sound in the Bonne Terre Public Library.

The click and whir of the big black ceiling fans. The silky brush of paper over the gleaming oak counters. The hum of computers. The scratch of pencils. The whisper of shoes across the old wood floors. On the second floor, a toddler shrieked and a mother quickly shushed him. There was the quiet beat of her heart and, of course, the not-so-quiet whispering of the high school students at the computer bank.

Owen Johns and his gang.

It was always Owen Johns and his gang.

Summer school had been moved from the high school to the library so they could finally fix the roof of the gymnasium. This meant Savannah had been looking at the smirking faces of Owen Johns, Garrett Watson and their various hangers-on for a week.

And in the days since the Manor had been violated, their smirks were smirkier, their eyes as they watched her a little too smug.

They did it.

She saw it in their eyes, the sour glee in their smiles, the dark triumph that wafted off them like stink from garbage. They'd torn apart her courtyard, her grandmother's orchids. Those boys had taken black spray paint to their stone walls, forcing her hand, and now there was a man at the Manor.

Matt Howe was in her home, in her courtyard, and Matt Howe made her heart pound and her stomach tremble and it was nearly intolerable.

And it was all Owen's and Garrett's fault.

She knew it with an instinct she didn't question. The O'Neill instinct—never wrong. The O'Neill impulses, on the other hand, too often lured by pounding hearts and trembling stomachs, were always disastrously wrong.

She stood at the counter and checked in the books from the overnight drop box. She traced the gilt beak of Mother Goose before shelving the faded red book on the trolley.

Her hands didn't shake. Her face didn't change, but she stood there, listening to their whispers, catching words like "she had a kid" and "he was married." She threw them, like logs, onto the fire of her anger.

She stood there as she had for years, calm and cool, pretending she didn't hear the whispers, and contemplated her revenge.

Not that she would take it. She'd learned her lesson about vengeance and acting on these O'Neill impulses. She'd learned it too well.

Ten years ago, maybe, she'd have enacted revenge. But now it was just an imaginary exercise. A highly satisfying one.

A letter to their parents, perhaps? Regarding some obscenely overdue books of a high monetary value? Good, but not quite enough.

"You watching the love triangle?" whispered Janice,

her assistant and Keeper of All Things Even Slightly Gossip-y.

"Love triangle?" Savannah whispered, keeping her eyes on Owen, Garrett and Owen's girlfriend.

"Owen's girlfriend," Janice whispered in the juicy tones of a soap addict, "I don't know her name, but I've been calling her The Cheerleader."

Savannah laughed; it was true, the redhead seemed incomplete without pom-poms.

"But The Cheerleader has been watching Garrett when Owen isn't looking."

"Really?" Savannah asked.

"And Garrett is not looking away."

Now *that* had the makings of revenge.

The phone rang and Janice waddled away to answer it while Savannah contemplated warm thoughts of love triangles blowing up.

"Hey!" Fingers snapped in front of Savannah's face and she jerked out of her fantasy to find her good friend Juliette Tremblant, looking stormy and all too police-chiefy across the counter.

"Hey, Juliette." Savannah smiled in the face of Juliette's stern expression. She was always, always happy to see her friend—even when Juliette was coming around to chastise her. "What's up?"

"What's up?" Juliette repeated, incredulously. Her black eyebrows practically hit her hairline. "You just hired some stranger to work at the Manor?"

"Word travels fast," Savannah said, amazed anew at the Bonne Terre interest in all things O'Neill. After twenty years she'd stopped being furious. Now she was merely irritated.

"One of my guys heard it from Wayne Smith who heard it from his wife who was taking her morning walk down your road and saw Margot and some stranger on the front porch shaking hands."

"Shh!" Owen and Garrett said, over-loud, over-annoying in mockery of Savannah's librarian battle cry.

"Excuse me?" Juliette turned to the boys, the badge clipped to the belt of her pants gleaming in the milky morning sunlight.

The boys went white and Savannah tried hard not to smile.

"Sorry, Chief Tremblant," they chorused and quickly returned to their work and summer school teacher.

"I need a badge," Savannah whispered.

"What you need is to have your head checked," Juliette said, her voice lower. "I called Margot this morning, to see if it was true and she said you'd hired a drifter. I guess living alone in that mausoleum has finally gotten to your heads, because that's not just notorious, it's dangerous."

"I don't know if he's a drifter," Savannah said, not entirely convinced he wasn't. And frankly, not entirely convinced that Juliette wasn't spot on in her assessment of Margot and Savannah.

"But he's not staying at the house. He's going to get a room at the Bonne Terre Inn."

"He's still a stranger," Juliette said.

"Right, and he's the only person who has answered that ad," Savannah pointed out. "Everyone in town who could do the work knows we don't have a big budget and that the job is huge."

"But a stranger?"

"I have vacation starting tomorrow—"

"And you're going to spend it babysitting this guy and your courtyard?"

"No, actually, I'm going to spend most of it doing research on extreme religious rituals around the world for the Discovery Channel, but I'll be home."

"What do you know about this guy?" Juliette asked, brushing her suit jacket off her lean hips, revealing her gun and her whipcord build.

Juliette looked so masculine, such a change from the girl she'd been. The girl, a few years older than Savannah, who had seemed the epitome of Southern glamour. Like a Creole Liz Taylor or something. Juliette used to never wear pants, and never left the house without a thick coat of hot-pink lip gloss.

Savannah wondered how much her brother Tyler had to do with the change in Juliette. Of course, that was years ago and Juliette would take her head off for asking.

"I checked his references," Savannah said, feeling confident until Juliette sniffed in disapproval. "And they were great."

"References lie," Juliette said.

"Give me some credit, Juliette. I'm a researcher. I searched his name on the Internet," she said, "and Matt Howe, at least the Matt Howe doing work at my house, hasn't been in the news for killing cats, or posting porn on the Web. He's a nonentity."

"Right, because the Internet is so reliable." Juliette pulled her notebook from her pocket and hit the end of her ballpoint pen. "Matt Howe?"

"With an *e*."

Juliette's pen scribbling across the lined paper added to the music of her library.

Juliette jabbed the notebook into her pocket. "What do you think of this guy, really?" Her eyes narrowed and Savannah shrugged.

"I don't like him. I don't want him in my house. But, I think he's safe. I think he's a good man."

"You've thought that before," Juliette whispered and Savannah flinched at the reminder. The reminder she didn't need.

"And I learned my lesson about handsome strangers, Juliette." She even managed to smile. "The O'Neills don't do love."

It was nearly imperceptible, but Juliette's right eyelid flinched.

"Juliette, I'm so sorr—"

"You guys have that island thing down pat. No one gets on and no one gets off," Juliette said. "At least not permanently."

Savannah shrugged. It was easier being alone. Safer. She wasn't going to apologize for it; it was a matter of survival.

"Margot managed to survive and some would say she's had more than her share of love," Juliette said.

"Business," Savannah clarified. People got confused about Margot all the time, thinking she was a romantic. She wasn't. She was a lusty capitalist with a penchant for the finer things in life. And men. "It was always business with Margot. And it's business with Matt Howe. You can trust me on that."

Juliette sniffed. "Okay, but I'm coming by tomorrow morning to check this guy out."

"You're welcome to," Savannah thought of the leonine grace of the man. The sharp predatory focus in his eyes. The way he pulled his khaki pants up over a lean waist, watching her as if he could taste her on his tongue.

Male. So thrillingly masculine among the roses and moss.

She'd spent so long pretending she wasn't a woman, pretending dark eyes and darker hair and a man with a knowing smile didn't send her to some place hot and internal. Someplace reckless and totally, entirely, O'Neill.

Stupidly, she found herself eager to get another look at Matt Howe, too.

MATT DIDN'T SLEEP MUCH anymore. The lure of the soft pillows and thick mattress of Bonne Terre Inn's room 3 no longer had much appeal for him. Instead he sat in the upright chair, watching the empty highway through the curtains.

In front of him was his sketch pad.

While waiting for Vanessa to show up, he was actually supposed to do some work.

He rotated the empty pad in quarter turns.

A blank page used to be a call to work, a spark to his imagination.

Now?

He remembered the kudzu. The destruction of the greenhouse. The tool shed in the back nearly obliterated by vines. The endless possibility of the space.

And he felt nothing. Just that cold breeze blowing through him that was growing increasingly familiar.

Thinking he could force it, the way he used to in college when he was so tired from exams his eyes felt like sandpaper, he framed out the perimeter, sketched in the existing buildings.

Sitting back he stared at his sketch, his work somehow familiar and foreign at the same time. How many of these had he done in his life? Rough sketches on napkins, on the backs of menus. He'd roughed out the working plan for the downtown warehouse renovations on the back of a pizza box. Then he'd taken that pizza box over to Jack's house in the middle of the night, so damn fired up about this plan. So damn blind with his own ambition.

He'd convinced his best friend to go in on the project with him, to be the civil engineer and contractor. He'd thought at the time it would be the professional adventure of a lifetime. For both of them.

Matt tried again to remember if Jack had said anything specific about that southwest corner. About choosing not to reinforce the floor, but he could not remember. Matt remembered Jack, dirty and stressed, saying that he couldn't take another loss, that the money was tight and his wife, Charlotte, was panicking, that the building was in worse shape than any of them had thought.

The lawyers had so easily absolved Matt of guilt, clapping their hands together and washing him clean of the tragedy all because he couldn't remember.

"But what if I'm lying?" he'd asked.

"Are you?"

He'd shaken his head, sick to his stomach, which was good enough for the lawyers.

But his sickness had stayed.

Disgusted with himself he stood, but felt shaky, as if he might vomit. When had he last eaten? A day ago? He ordered pizza and spent the rest of the night focused on Savannah and her secrets until finally the sky was turned gray, pink at the edges, and a new day had come to save him from the night.

After grabbing a coffee at the bakery next door he drove toward the O'Neill house, but as he turned left onto the country road to the Manor, he slid on his glasses, because, in the distance, it appeared a police cruiser was parked out front.

With its lights on.

Was Vanessa back?

Were Savannah and Margot guilty of crimes like Vanessa?

A wicked anticipation and something painful bit into Matt's stomach. Was this it? Was he going to arrive only to see Savannah and Margot being led away in chains?

The statute of limitations for the theft of the jewels was past, so they couldn't be arrested for that.

Were they being arrested for something else?

Was this how Justice corrected her aim?

His foot pressed on the accelerator, dust flying up behind him in his rearview mirror.

The duality of it was perfect, though he had to admit there was something in him that balked at the idea of Savannah's cool beauty in a hot desperate cell like his father's.

But if it was what she deserved, then so be it.

Do the crime, do the time, as his father always said.

He braked to a hard stop just behind the cruiser and threw himself out the door. No press. No throngs of cops. Just one cruiser with its lights going and the old house, looking sadder in the bright morning sunlight.

Matt found everyone in the living room where it was still cool and dark, the windows shadowed by the veranda out front. The cops he expected to see leading the women away sat in spindly Queen Anne chairs, dropping sugar from their beignets onto the faded upholstery.

Margot stood beside a frayed velveteen couch, her hand gripping Savannah's shoulder.

Savannah sat holding a little girl as if her whole life depended on it, the child's red head buried in Savannah's neck.

Matt rocked to a stop in the doorway.

A little girl?

How had he missed that in his investigation? Why hadn't Savannah told him when he asked?

It shouldn't change anything, but it did.

Seeing Savannah with a little girl clinging to her neck as if any moment she might be torn away opened up a giant hole in his chest.

He remembered holding on to his father's neck the same way, as if the cancer might pounce and take his dad from him.

And suddenly he didn't want to witness Savannah being led away in chains, not if it meant the girl had to witness it, as well.

"I don't think it was high-schoolers," Savannah said, staring daggers at the two cops with poor eating habits. "They've never tried to break into the house before."

"Well," one of the cops said, brushing his hands together and readjusting his girth in the small chair. "It was only a matter of time before some kid got bold enough to try it."

"I'm sure it's another prank," the thin cop said.

"A prank!" Savannah nearly yelled. "You guys have looked the other way for years, and we've accepted that as part of the price of living here and being an O'Neill. But someone tried to break into my daughter's room. It's the hardest room to get to from the outside and it's not even accessible from the back courtyard."

The rage and fear in Savannah's eyes were real and hot enough to bend steel.

"We've dusted for prints and we'll see what it turns up," Thin Cop said.

"And then?" Savannah asked, practically spitting fire. Matt could understand her ire. These men were not taking her seriously; their disdain was practically written on the walls. Suddenly, Margot's comment about the O'Neills being a target around here took on painful ramifications.

"And then, if possible, we'll make some arrests," Thin Cop said.

"And what will you be doing in the meantime? To help protect us as citizens of Bonne Terre? Which, I can't believe I need to remind you, is your job."

"Look, if you want a man out front, you're going to have to take that up with Chief Tremblant—"

"Which I will," Savannah said, standing with the little girl clinging to her like a monkey. "Now, I'd—"

"We'd like to thank you gentlemen for your hard work." Margot stepped in, like a gracious host or a bomb expert.

"You know," Fat Cop said, his beady eyes glued to Savannah as if she were the one guilty of breaking into her daughter's room, "word in town is you've hired some stranger to do work around here."

Matt opened his mouth, but Savannah was there before him. "What are you getting at, Officer Jones?"

"If you don't want trouble, don't ask for it." His tone oozed a sexual patronization that made Matt want to put his fist in the big man's face. "Seems to me you O'Neills have had a hard time learning that lesson. Maybe that's why we're not bending over to make sure y'all are safe and sound. You could take better care your damn selves."

Enough was enough, and Matt stepped out of the shadowed doorway.

"I'm not here to hurt these women," he said and all eyes swung to him. He met the cops head-on and could feel Savannah staring at him with his whole body.

What he said, of course, wasn't totally true, but Matt was living in the dark edges between truth and perception. But he wasn't here to hurt them like this—scaring children and mothers in the middle of the night.

"Then you'll have no problem telling me your where-abouts last night," Fat Cop said.

"Room 3 at the Bonne Terre Inn. All night."

"Any witnesses to that fact?"

"I ordered a pizza at midnight."

"Break-in was at two."

"I took my box out to the garbage around that time. I waved to Mrs. Adams at the front desk." He put his fists on his hips to keep them from going to work on the guy's nose and smug grin. "I'm not here to hurt anyone," he reiterated, glancing sideways at Savannah to see if she got the message.

She stared at him, her eyes thick blue wells of anger and worry. For a moment, a millisecond, he saw the girlfriend of the man—boy, really—who'd died, whose blood was all over Matt's hands.

The room dipped around him. Time collapsed and that point-seven seconds nearly got him.

"Come on, Jim," Thin Cop said, putting a hand on his partner's beefy shoulder. Matt focused on them as hard as he could, shoving away his memories of the girlfriend and her pain. "We're going to find out it was Owen and his friends, we both know it. Let's leave these people alone."

Officer Jones gave Matt a long look then turned to Savannah. "You. Both of you—" he glanced at Margot, raking the two women with his eyes "—you're just like Vanessa."

Savannah went white and Matt didn't think, he simply acted, stepping in between Savannah and the policeman.

"It's time for you to go," Matt said.

It took a moment of hard stare-down between Matt and Officer Jones but finally the cop nodded, slicked back his thinning hair and slid his hat on. "We'll be in touch," he said, barely looking at the women standing around the couch. Instead he took a careful step toward Matt, who tensed, every muscle suddenly eager for a fight.

"I'll be watching you," the man murmured.

"That'll be fun," Matt said with a smirk, guaranteed to piss off the cop. And it did. Luckily, his partner got a hand around the guy's arm and led him out of the house before violence erupted.

"Oh, my," Margot said, once the cops were gone. She collapsed onto the blue velveteen couch, a puddle of white linen and silk. "That was more than I needed this morning."

"I didn't like those police officers," the little girl said, lifting her head from her mother's neck.

"You and me both," Margot said, holding out her arms and the girl climbed from mother to great-grandmother.

Savannah didn't say anything, just glared at him as if it were his judgment day.

"It wasn't me," he said, even though he knew it didn't matter. She either believed him or not.

"I know that," Savannah answered, her voice rough and husky, no doubt from swallowing so much anger, and his shoulders went down, his back got loose with relief.

He noticed her robe, purple silk with Asian style hand-painted flowers gliding over her breasts, tied tight at her trim waist. No wonder Fat Cop was leering—Matt was in danger of doing it himself. The prison warden from yesterday was long gone and in her place was something far more dangerous.

A woman with a lit fuse.

Christ, he wanted to touch her.

Her hair was down. Her face clean and clear of makeup, her skin like the inside of a seashell. And her eyes...well, her big blue forthright eyes were killing him.

"What happened?" he asked.

"Around two this morning, Katie started screaming." Savannah sighed, rubbing her forehead. "I ran in there and saw someone jumping out her window."

"Oh, my God," he whispered, imagining that to be a parent's worst nightmare. "Was she...is she hurt?"

"No." The redheaded girl spoke up, pushing back long tangles of hair to reveal freckles and blue eyes. "I'm not. I was just scared."

"Do you know why anyone would try to get into the house?" he asked, studying Savannah carefully for any indication that there was a safe somewhere filled with jewels.

Savannah shook her head, looking slightly lost.

"Is there anything of value—"

"That's hardly any of your business," Margot said, and he tore his eyes away from Savannah to look at her, stunned to see that without the careful application of makeup, her face really showed her age. "Nor is it polite conversation at 7:00 a.m."

Matt ducked his head. "Sorry," he murmured. "I apologize."

"I do, too," Margot said graciously after Savannah shot her a stern look. "It's been a rough morning. But it probably *was* those teenagers." Margot sighed, resting her head against the back of the settee. "The officers are right, it was only a matter of time—"

"Those officers were idiots," Savannah snapped. "Someone broke into my daughter's room and they acted like it was nothing." Savannah's voice broke and she turned away from her daughter as if to hide her runaway emotions.

Something dented in Matt's chest, a foundation trembled and he wanted to reach out and touch the fragile elegant bones of her wrist. Hold her hand.

Ruthlessly, he looked around the room, turning himself off to the emotions, embracing the chill that lived inside of him.

Do not get attached to these women, he told himself.

"Thank you," Savannah said and he swung around to look at her, made speechless for a moment by her beauty, by the look in her eyes. "For what you said to those officers."

There was something slightly different in her, a fierceness transformed. It was as if a light had gone on in a dark house. His conscience, quiet for so long, muted and grieving, woke up.

Don't do this, he thought. *Don't look at me like that. Don't let me in, I'm only here to hurt you.*

"No problem," he said.

"Who are you?" a small voice asked, and he turned to see the girl giving him the once-over.

Matt's lip lifted at the quicksilver change in topics. "My name is Matt, I'm going to help fix the back garden."

Katie's eyes narrowed and she harrumphed, looking as skeptical as a young girl could, which, actually, was pretty damn skeptical.

"He's going to be staying here. In the sleeping porch. At night," Margot said, and she might as well have shot off a cannon into the silent room.

CHAPTER FOUR

SAVANNAH LOOKED DUMBSTRUCK. She blinked. Blinked again. Matt resisted taking a step back, away from her.

"I'm sorry?" she finally said.

"He's staying," Margot repeated, showing a whole lot of that steel under her magnolia exterior. "I know, I know." She waved her hands in Savannah's face as it grew stormier by the second. "You told him to stay at the Inn, but I told him he could stay on the sleeping porch and frankly, after what's happened, I think it's a damn good idea to have a man around here."

"What?" Savannah cried. "This is not the Wild West, Margot."

"No, but it's our home and I'm eighty and Katie's eight and you're a damn librarian. We're about as defenseless as it gets."

"We could get a gun," Katie said and both Savannah and Margot spun to stare at her. "I'm just saying," she added sheepishly.

"We're not getting a gun," Margot said. "Matt is sleeping on the porch. End of story."

"Can I talk to you?" Savannah said through her teeth. "Privately."

"No, you can't. You're too wrapped up in the past and the last man who stayed here."

Savannah went stiff and pale as ice and Matt had to

fight himself not to show a reaction. What last man? And what did he do?

"You can't see that this is a perfect solution to our problem," Margot said.

Savannah spun toward Matt, not even pretending to smile or be gracious. "Can you give us a minute?"

"Sure."

"Stay right there," Margot said, pointing a finger to the floor in front of Matt's feet. He wouldn't have moved even if the earth opened up and tried to swallow him. "Look, we're targets around here. The police don't much care for us for a bunch of different reasons, not the least of which is they're giant dickheads—sorry, Katie."

"It's okay," Katie said, as though she was taking in the greatest show on earth.

"The police chief is good to us, but she's got a whole town to take care of. So, we're pretty much on our own," Margot said. "Savannah's got a problem with men staying here—"

"Don't you dare, Margot," Savannah snapped.

"Because we've been alone a long time." She held up one elegant finger. "By choice, mind you. Most of the time men are only good for two things, and one of them is buying me drinks."

Matt choked back a laugh. What in the world had he stumbled into?

"But…I'm scared," Margot admitted. "We all are." The air in the room seemed to change, a heavy darkness filling the corners, creeping along the floor, the specter of what might have happened last night. Margot's eyes, suddenly damp, turned to Savannah. "I think if Matt were to stay, maybe we could all sleep instead of worrying who was going to break into our house, or might come looking for us in the night."

Savannah and Margot looked at each other for a long time, the kind of silent communication he understood some people had with each other. He turned away, the moment suddenly too intimate to bear witness to, especially when he was lying to them.

"Do you want to stay here?" Savannah asked him.

"I want to help," he said, keeping his real motivation to himself. His quest for justice was his little secret, the heartbeat that kept him moving, and more access to this house and its secrets would only be a good thing. "It's why you hired me. And if I spent the night, I could get a lot more work done."

"We can't pay you more," Savannah said. "But with the money you'd be saving—"

"It works out fine. Truth is," he said with a shrug, unsure of where these words were coming from and why he was saying them, "I don't sleep much. So, it really doesn't matter."

"Fine," Savannah said, squeezing her hands together, but not before Matt saw them tremble. "It's settled. Matt, welcome to the Manor."

KATIE SPENT THE MORNING on Savannah's lap, which didn't bother her mother one bit. Savannah was actually dueling with the instinct to somehow chain her daughter to her side.

If something had happened... She squelched the thought, as she had a thousand times already this morning, and pressed a kiss to her daughter's head. The sun was sliding past high noon and fear and worry were beginning to chase each other in small circles in her stomach.

What nightmare would tonight bring?

She already knew she wouldn't be sleeping. Probably

not for the next few nights. And not only because of the break-in.

There was a man in her house.

Margot played dirty. She always did. Going behind Savannah's back that way and giving Matt the sleeping porch—classic Margot maneuvering. But Savannah couldn't argue this time. Because Margot *was* right. Things were different around the Manor. The pranks, if they were high school pranks, had turned ugly. Suspicious. Having someone keeping watch was smart.

"We can't even play hide-and-seek," Katie moaned, looking out the window over Savannah's printer to the courtyard below. "That man is there."

Savannah tried not to look, but Matt was a magnet and she had all the willpower of iron shavings.

The gray T-shirt clinging to his back was nearly black with sweat, and his dark brown hair was wet and thick against his strong neck. Through her open window it seemed the wind carried his scent to her, sweat, sunshine and wood.

The urge to close her eyes and inhale, to stick out her tongue just a little bit and taste the air that had touched him nearly overcame her.

She'd been in control of these sudden cravings, this outrageous lust that had taken root in her body, but at some point midmorning, Matt had put on glasses.

Glasses.

Which added a spice to Matt that was infinitely appealing. At least to Savannah. The librarian in her liked bookish men. Bookish men with the shoulders and biceps of men used to doing hard work.

This was worse than inappropriate. These ridiculous feelings she had for him were flat-out wrong. Wrong because he worked for her and wrong because he was a stranger and wrong because…well, just wrong.

He was going to be staying here. Downstairs. A hundred yards from where she slept. It had been years since someone other than Katie and Margot had shared this house with her.

She didn't know if she was grateful for his presence or sick over it.

"Yes, he is there," she said. And oddly, the thought was comforting. As well as really unnerving. And a little exciting.

He was a guard dog. A big one. And considering the events of the morning, she'd even say he was a good one.

"I thought he was going to punch Officer Jones in the face," bloodthirsty Katie said, her eyes sparkling. "Pow." She illustrated a hard little punch with her closed fist.

Savannah caught it and kissed the little knuckles, hard and smooth like diamonds under flesh. "It was a bit intense, wasn't it?"

Savannah had thought the same. As she'd stood there, watching Matt, a stranger to them, jump to their defense, she'd actually wished he *would* hit Officer Jones. Officer Jones who apparently still hadn't gotten over his high school dumping at Vanessa's hands.

We just can't get a break, she thought. The O'Neill curse was riding them particularly hard this summer. The vandalism, the break-in.

Again she looked at Matt, wondering somehow if he was here to balance the scales for them. Something sweet for all the bitter they'd been eating.

Honest to God help.

It seemed unimaginable.

They'd been alone, the three of them, for so long.

There had to be a catch. The universe didn't send blessings to the O'Neills without payment of some kind.

"I'm going to go get something to eat," Katie said, scrambling off Savannah's numb knees.

"Good idea," she said, clearing her screen of the computer games they'd been playing. Work, she thought, it was time to focus on work. To clear away every other distraction and chase information across the World Wide Web.

Knights Templar, she thought. Warriors and protectors. She'd start there.

But her gaze strayed outside. To Matt.

Her blood was beginning to buzz, the O'Neill curse manifesting itself in her the way it always did. Curiosity. God, it killed her every time. She could bury it, channel it into her job. Research every natural disaster in the southern hemisphere before the 1700s. Find every voodoo use for frog blood.

But right now she wanted to go out there and research their new handyman. Why was he here? Why did he want to stay? To help?

She shook her head, gritted her teeth and fought down her urge to go outside and watch him. Talk to him.

Chaining herself to her work, to her desk and the small oasis that was her life, Savannah, as she always did, suppressed what was O'Neill in her.

But she had to wonder, feeling herself pull against the self-imposed bonds, how long could she hold out?

IT WAS LATE AFTERNOON. Matt could tell by the thickness and heft of the sunlight hitting what remained of the greenhouse—a cement pad. That's it.

He stripped off his gloves and wiped his dripping forehead with the sleeve of his shirt. Useless, considering the saturation of that sleeve. The whole shirt, actually.

Good God, it was hot. So hot the air was thick in his throat and prickles of heat crawled up and down his legs under sweat-soaked jeans.

His socks were wet. It was disgusting.

He hadn't done this kind of labor since he'd worked for that civil engineer during college. His shoulders and back weren't really enjoying it, but the effort felt good. Clean, somehow.

There were worse ways to wait for Vanessa to show up, and it sure as hell beat watching the four walls of his condo close in around him.

Scrap still needed to be carried out to the curb, but now he could get to work on making sure the back wall was safe—the farthest corner had slid apart into a loose heap.

There was a kid living here, for crying out loud. And this courtyard was like a death trap.

He felt eyes on the back of his neck and he sighed. Seriously, that little girl was getting to be a pest. Not that she did anything, or said anything. She simply watched him.

It was creeping him out.

"Katie—"

"It's Savannah." Oh, man, was it ever. Even the sound of her voice sent blood pounding through his veins. He turned and saw her in the shadows under the cypress. "Has Katie been bothering you?"

He smiled and shook his head. "She's just curious."

"Curious." Savannah actually smiled. "Is that another word for pain in the butt?"

"I was thinking precocious."

Savannah nodded, calm and cool as if it wasn't a million degrees outside and suddenly Matt felt every drop of sweat on his body. "Everything okay?" she asked. "You... ah...finding stuff?"

He looked down at the ancient sledgehammer and even older hand tools that he'd found in the shed. An upgrade would be needed if he was going to get this courtyard done with the skin of his hands intact.

"Sure," he said. "But I think tomorrow I'll go into town and get some supplies."

"You'll need money?"

He shook his head, guilt eating away at him. He was lying, and now he was taking their money. "Margot gave me a deposit." Not that he would ever cash the check.

She paused, standing there as if there was something more she wanted to say. It made him nervous, the way she simply stood, watching him, as though she saw right through his bad smoke screen. As though she knew why he was here.

And frankly, he was dying to ask about Vanessa. The questions were beating against his teeth, but it was too soon. Savannah was so suspicious already, and there was no way he could bring the subject of her mother up and make it seem natural. He needed to bide his time, wait for his moment.

"What's your plan out here?" she asked.

"Well, I'm going to start on the stone wall next." He wiped his forehead and pointed over to the corner where the wall had crumbled.

"You're bleeding."

He glanced down at his arms and found a hundred little cuts and slices that he hadn't even felt until this moment. "It's fine. Glass."

Savannah looked as if she were going to argue, but then she nodded.

The silence was thick. Uncomfortable. The tension more dense than the humid air.

"There's nothing to steal here, you know that, right?" she asked and he nearly dropped the shovel.

"I'm sorry?"

"If you're thinking about robbing us, I'm just letting you know, in case you missed it, there's nothing worth stealing. Hasn't been for years."

There was something very sad behind her eyes, behind her words and he tried to resist it. "You always this forthright?"

"Saves time," she said, shrugging, and stepped over to the rock slide that made up the closest corner of the wall. She kicked at a small stone, sending it clattering across its larger brethren.

"I'm not here to rob you," he assured her. Forthright, sure. And suspicious as all get-out.

"Then why are you here?" she asked, watching him through her thick fall of hair. Straight as glass that hair, like a curtain, and he got the distinct impression that she spent a lot of time watching people from behind it.

"I thought we already covered this," he asked, not wanting to go back over his lies. Not wanting to talk to her at all, actually. It made him feel slimy, less righteous and more like a liar. He didn't need that.

"Right." She nodded and climbed up on another rock and turned to face him. Her daughter had done the exact same thing a few hours ago. This was a new side to Savannah, something he didn't expect. Something playful. Young. "You're a good Samaritan here to help Louisiana one crumbling courtyard at a time."

Her wit matched her sharp beauty and he liked that. Liked that more and more about her, but wondered what softness, what sadness that sharp wit protected. "Something like that. You want to help me move some of those rocks?"

She shook her head, climbed up higher. "It's what we're paying you the big bucks for. You know, people leave their homes because they're running from something."

Matt's sweat dried up and went cold. "I assume you're talking about me?"

"A lot of the world—it's basic human nature."

"What if I'm looking for something?" he asked, looking her right in the eye, gauging her reaction.

Something electric filled the air between them. Something more dangerous than lies. More trouble than gems. Something hot and deep and compelling.

I want her, he thought, suddenly hungry for the taste of her pink lips. And he realized, looking at her, that she was out here because she wanted him, too.

CHAPTER FIVE

SAVANNAH WAS A FLY IN AMBER. She couldn't move. Couldn't look away. Matt's green eyes blazed and her flesh tingled, pulsed.

She jerked, reining herself in. It was stupid to come out here. Total O'Neill stupidity. She should have known better, she should have stayed in her room and kept working.

"Well," she finally said, jumping down from the rocks on the other side of the pile, away from him. She turned her back, trying to get her bearings. Her breath. "Whatever you're looking for, you won't find it here."

"Tell me something." His voice was deep and rich, like coffee. She loved coffee. "This thing with the cops? Why aren't they taking this seriously?"

"It's an old grudge," she said, turning around to give him the Cliff's Notes. "O'Neills have run brothels, bootlegging operations and part of the underground railroad out of this house. Cops don't like us and we're not always fond of them."

"Your grandmother seems pretty law abiding," he said.

She laughed, lulled into a conversation she usually hated. "She's the worst of them all. Well, not the worst, I suppose. My brother Tyler might be."

"What about your mother?"

She supposed it was natural, that he would wonder about her mother, a bunch of women in a house together with one generation missing. But it didn't mean she had to answer him.

She picked up a rock and tossed it over the fence, ignoring him.

"And your dad?" he asked. "Or are men not allowed?"

"You're here."

He nodded, smiled slightly. "I guess I should be glad."

The silence buzzed as if carrying the weight of all his unasked questions, and she could actually feel him thinking. Wondering.

"What was it that Tyler did to make things so bad?" he finally asked.

"He dated the police chief's daughter," she said. "Broke her heart. For years, anything went wrong in town, anything at all and the first person they'd talk to was an O'Neill."

"That's not fair," he said, stiff and stern as though he knew what was fair in this world.

"Whatever is?" she asked, facing him. After a moment he nodded, as if he understood that nothing was fair. Nothing at all. And once again she had that niggling feeling in her head that this man was not all that he seemed.

Were they fools? she wondered. Trusting this man? This stranger?

What would it cost them, in the end, to trust him now?

"What about you?" he asked, his voice light, as though he was teasing her. "Did you get into trouble?"

Her breath clogged in her throat, turned into a rock she had to try to swallow.

"I'm an O'Neill," she said, with a stiff shrug. "It's what we do."

Savannah tried to step over the rocks and head toward the house and the safety of her room, but distracted and skittish, she tilted off balance.

"Watch it," Matt murmured, his hand a brand at her waist. She sucked in a quick breath and twisted away, stumbling slightly across the rocks, but she made it to solid ground.

Her waist still burned, the flesh scorched and tingling.

He was close, too close. She could see the black and brown in his eyes, flecks of gold.

"I'm trusting you," she said. "In my home. The home where my daughter sleeps. My grandmother. And it's not an easy thing to do."

"I understand," he said, as if he really did and wouldn't that be something.

"My family—" She started but didn't know how to put it all into words—their past, her fears. She smiled but it felt broken at the corners, as if the weight of happiness, of hope, was simply too much to hold.

The sunlight hit his face, turned his hair to sable and his eyes to polished glass.

She was sucker punched by his beauty and his strength.

"Don't hurt us," she finally whispered. "Don't hurt us more than we've been hurt."

AFTER DINNER, Savannah sat on the front porch drinking iced tea and waited for Juliette, who had called to say she was coming over with word about fingerprints.

She was also trying to avoid Matt. A little too late, she knew, after this afternoon. She should never have given in to her curiosity and gone down to talk to him.

Her waist still felt his touch, like a shadow or a burn.

It was so strange having a man around. In this house of estrogen and silk, the deep timbre of a man's voice hadn't been heard after dinner for eight years.

It made her miss her brothers. She should contact them, tell them to come home for Christmas. It was time. This distance between them, growing and growing over the years, was too much. Tyler avoiding this town like the plague and Carter being too busy to spend some time with family, it had to end, or this distance would grow into something worse. Something they wouldn't be able to get over at a Christmas dinner.

They'd be strangers to each other and she couldn't bear that.

Matt walked past, his arms filled with scrap metal and wood from the back courtyard that he dumped by the side of the road.

So much for avoiding him. He lifted his hand in a wave and she nodded, feeling stiff and foolish like a sixteen-year-old girl with a crush.

Juliette pulled up in her tan sedan and Savannah was glad for the distraction.

"So?" Juliette said, joining her on the porch steps as Matt went around the house to the courtyards. She stretched out her long legs and leaned back against the railing. "That's Matt Howe?"

"That's him."

"Where's Katie?"

"In the kitchen with Margot. They're baking away their stress. You should stick around for sugar pie."

"I will," Juliette said. "You thinking about shagging away your stress?" Juliette asked, nodding in the direction Matt had disappeared. Savannah laughed. "It's not funny, Savannah, you're staring at that man like *he's* the sugar pie."

"Don't be ridiculous," Savannah said, blushing and angry because she knew Juliette was right. Worse, she would have to admit about Matt's sleeping arrangements. And Juliette was never going to believe Savannah didn't want to have sex with him. "Matt is spending the night here now."

"Where?"

"Sleeping porch." Juliette opened her mouth to protest and Savannah held up her hand. "You don't have the staff to stake out my house and I've already hired the man to be around. Might as well have him around the clock."

"I've called in some favors with the boys in Baton Rouge," Juliette said, "they're gonna run Matt's name through the computer up there."

"That would be fine." They wouldn't find anything, Savannah thought.

Juliette smiled. "But not necessary?"

"I trust him, don't ask me why."

"You trusted Eric."

Right. Eric. The mistake by which all other mistakes were measured. "Everyone wants to talk about Eric these days," Savannah muttered.

"For good reason," Juliette said. "History might be repeating itself before our very eyes."

"I was already sleeping with Eric before I invited him to stay here. And I'm not sleeping with Matt. I'm not doing anything with Matt."

"Except watching him from the porch."

Savannah sighed. "Nothing wrong with that."

Matt emerged once more from behind the house, his arms full, muscles flexed and damp. "Not when he looks like that," Juliette said. "Good lord. Glasses?"

"*I know.*" Savannah smiled. "I don't think ax murderers wear glasses, do they?"

"That's not at all funny," Juliette grumbled.

Savannah turned to her friend and slid her hand over Juliette's elbow. "Thank you for being here last night," Savannah said, reliving those terrifying moments after Katie's screams had split the night. She'd called Juliette, frantic and freaked out, and her friend had arrived in no time, stayed until the fingerprints had been dusted, then rushed them to the station and all the fancy equipment she'd purchased last year.

"I'm glad you called," Juliette said, squeezing Savannah's fingers. "I'm just sorry I don't have more information for you."

Savannah braced herself. "The fingerprints?"

"The only prints in the whole room were yours, Margot's and Katie's. The intruder must have been wearing gloves."

"The high school kids who wreck our property don't seem the type to wear gloves."

"You don't think it was a kid?"

"It was so dark," Savannah murmured, wishing she'd seen more. Wishing there was more she could do to protect her daughter, her home. She closed her eyes, imagining the windowsill, the bright moon glinting off blond hair as the person climbed back out the window. "All I saw was blond hair."

"Well, without fingerprints…"

"I know. It probably *was* Owen or Garrett, they're both blond and I'm sure they're the ones who destroyed the greenhouse and painted the graffiti on the walls."

"I'll go have a word with their parents," Juliette said. "See if we can't get them to do a better job with their parenting skills."

"I don't think that's in the police chief job description," Savannah said, quirking her eyebrow at Juliette.

"It's a small town," Juliette said with a shrug. "I can make this stuff up as I go. But look, if it wasn't a kid and someone is targeting this house, I need you to call me if you see anything suspicious. Anything at all."

"Absolutely."

"And keep an eye on that Matt guy."

"No problem."

Juliette smirked. "Clearly."

Savannah laughed, for the first time in what felt like days. Just then, Juliette's phone buzzed at her hip.

"You want that pie?" Savannah asked.

"Save some for me," Juliette said, unclipping her phone from her belt. "I gotta go. I'll call you later."

Savannah waved and watched Juliette, phone to her ear, rushing off to take care of important business. Pressing issues. Fingerprints and parents and juvenile delinquents.

Savannah's life seemed at that moment to exist on the head of a pin. She had Katie. Margot. The library. Faceless clients and a secure Internet connection. She'd liked it that way, wanted it that way.

After Eric had come into her life and destroyed so much, she'd done everything in her power to shrink her exposure to the outside world down to practically nothing. Her oasis. But the outside world still forced itself upon her. It broke into her house. Threatened her family.

The clatter of wood and metal snapped her head around. Matt stood at the edge of the lawn, watching her.

"You okay?" he asked, tilting his head. Sunlight glinted off his glasses, obliterating his eyes.

She nodded, unsure of what she would say if she opened her mouth.

IT TOOK TWO DAYS to finally get to the hardware store because he got distracted by the cobblestones and breaking up the concrete pad.

He'd also tried his damnedest to get any one of the O'Neill women to talk to him about Vanessa.

But they weren't talking.

Even Katie, when he'd asked her about her grandmother, had given him a blank look and left.

All this led him to believe that Vanessa hadn't come here yet. And he had to wonder if she planned on just waltzing in here, because it was obvious she wouldn't be very welcome.

Bright and early on Wednesday, Matt drove into town and found the hardware store. It was well-stocked for a town this size and what he couldn't put in his cart—the tiller, chain saw and sod—he was able to have delivered.

"We can get you two more bags of cement," the old man behind the counter said, his red plaid shirt straining at the buttons over his belly. "In fact, let me check in the warehouse, sometimes we keep overflow there."

"Great," Matt said, and the man tucked his pencil behind his ear and left. Matt started piling up the hand tools, gloves and nails on the counter, but jumped when a woman slid into the old man's spot.

"You that man working out at the Manor?" she asked, her long gray hair pulled into a ponytail, her eyes, behind glasses, bright and focused. Rabid, nearly.

"That would be me," he said, cautiously.

"I told you, Doug!" she yelled, and another man, a younger version of the man in red plaid, appeared at her elbow.

"So?" she asked. "Is it true what they say?"

Matt blinked. "What exactly do they say?"

"That Margot's crazy," the woman said.

"And Savannah's a slut," Doug said bitterly, and the woman slapped his arm.

"Watch yourself," she said. "There's no need for name calling."

Doug didn't for a second seem sheepish and Matt had the urge to teach the boy some manners with his fists, but he realized an opportunity when he saw one.

If the O'Neills wouldn't talk about the O'Neills, maybe he could get his news from another source. And there was nothing as far-reaching as small-town gossip.

"They seem fine enough," he answered, leaning against the counter as if settling in for a nice chat. "My name is Matt."

"Cheryl," she said, smiling. "This is my boy, Doug."

"Nice to meet you," he said, pouring it on a little thick, but Cheryl seemed to eat it up. "Now what's this about Margot being crazy?"

"Well, people been saying it for years, that Margot buries money in the backyard."

"No, I heard she stopped doing that," Doug said. "On account of all those high schoolers who go back there to party."

"You know that Garrett boy broke into the house, scared those women to pieces."

Matt took note of the name and watched as the two seemed to forget he was there.

"Can you blame him?" Doug asked. "I wish I had the guts to get close to that house. I heard they've got this huge wall safe in the library filled with gems."

"Well, honey, if you'd been nicer to Savannah, maybe Margot wouldn't have run you off when you tried," Cheryl said and Doug rolled his eyes.

But the hair on Matt's neck stood up and chill washed

over his arms. "Gems?" he asked blankly, steering them back on course.

"Diamonds and such. Big ones. Can you imagine?"

Yes, he thought. He could. He did.

"Where would they get gems?" he asked. "I mean, judging from the house, those two women are barely getting by."

"Don't be fooled," Doug said, starting to ring up the items in front of him. "It's all a cover."

Cheryl nodded and Matt glanced between them. "Cover for what?"

"I think it's the middle boy, Tyler," Doug said. "I don't know how, but I think they're hiding the money he wins in Vegas so he doesn't have to pay taxes."

Cheryl shook her head. "I think it's the mother, what's her name—"

"Vanessa?" Matt asked, perhaps a bit too eagerly, but Cheryl didn't seem to notice. "But where is she?" he asked. "They never talk about her."

"Oh, God, no." Doug laughed. "No one talks about Vanessa. Ever. Savannah about slapped my head off a few years ago when I asked her."

Matt paused a moment, grateful that Savannah had ignored him rather than slapped his head off.

"I told you that was no way to get her to go out with you." Cheryl tsked her tongue and Matt got a little insight into that slut comment. A beautiful woman like Savannah who wouldn't date the riffraff—what else would the riffraff do but call her names?

Something detonated in his chest, sympathy and anger that there was no one around to defend these women against people bent on believing the worst of them.

You, he thought, *you could do it.*

But he wasn't here to defend them, not any more than

he had. He was here for answers and so far, Cheryl and Doug had been more help than all three O'Neill women combined.

"So where is Vanessa?" Matt asked, even though he knew. Or had known.

"No one's seen her in years," Doug said.

"Oh," Cheryl laughed. "Just because she ain't been seen doesn't mean she's not around. Trouble, that one. Worse than all the others put together. Her and that husband of hers."

Matt's head spun. "Husband?"

"Richard someone or other. He and Vanessa got divorced long before the kids ended up in Bonne Terre."

There was a thump behind them, the old man in the red shirt reappeared and Cheryl vanished like a ghost.

"That will be two hundred twelve dollars and thirty-two cents," Doug said. Matt blinked, stunned to see all of his stuff in bags and Doug smiling at him as if he hadn't been saying the foulest things about Savannah moments ago.

"Hold on there, Doug. Add two bags of ready-mix," the old man said, then turned to Matt. "You'll have to go around back to get them."

"Ah…no problem," Matt said and took out his wallet.

"I got it from here, Doug, thanks," the man said and Doug walked off. He said he was going to check on fishing rods, but the safe bet was Doug finding mommy and doing what they did best.

Matt put his money on the counter but the old guy ignored it, looking hard into Matt's eyes.

"Don't listen to my family," he said. "Those O'Neill women are good people. Don't deserve what's been done to them."

Don't hurt us. Don't hurt us more than we've been hurt.
"What's been done to them?"

"They been left, boy. Time and time again, they been left and that will make a person do some crazy things."

THE NIGHT HAD A TEXTURE TO IT, a lush throbbing weight that reminded Matt that there were a lot of living things out in all that blackness. Living things like snakes. Alligators. Big bugs that he wasn't real fond of. And the only thing between him and them was the thin metal screen of the sleeping porch.

It hadn't seemed quite as bad the past few nights, but he'd been falling asleep so hard and so deep it was as if he'd died.

Tonight, his head was spinning, trying to separate malicious gossip and rumor from what might possibly be the truth.

The gems, here?

Christ, it would make his life a whole lot easier. And, frankly, it explained why the kids were always breaking into the back courtyard. Why the greenhouse was destroyed and why suddenly someone was bold enough to try to get into the house.

Why they wanted a security camera in their garden.

Gems, thousands of dollars in a wall safe.

People did worse for less.

Like you, he thought, guilt eating at the edges of his mind.

He should have said something to Doug, a little something to keep his mouth shut about Savannah. But he hadn't. He'd walked away and now he was going to use Doug's gossip against them.

I'm no better than Doug. I'm worse.

He turned on the small camping lantern that Margot had given him because the porch wasn't wired with electricity. The white sheets on the narrow cot glowed, and other than some gardening pots in the corner of the room where he'd hidden the surveillance photos and files, the porch was empty.

No wall safes. No gems.

Bugs were attracted to the light and buzzed against the screens, beating giant wings against the metal.

Freaked out, he turned off the light, opting for the ghostly half-light of the moon.

Room 3 at Bonne Terre Inn was getting more appealing by the minute.

But there were no chances to study the lovely, wounded and Notorious O'Neill women in room three.

Don't hurt us any more than we've been hurt.

Why did she have to say that?

Why did he have to feel guilty for doing what was right for his dad? His father, who had been hung out to dry by Vanessa and Richard.

He checked his watch. Dad called him every Wednesday at this time. Jail was a lonely place and these weekly calls were important. To both of them. Joel Woods may not have been the best father, but he'd done the best he could.

Matt grabbed his cell phone, depressed the power button under his thumb and the annoying chime of an activated phone sounded loud in the quiet night.

"Hello, Matt," his phone said. "You have twenty voice mail messages."

He groaned and looked down at the display. Erica. Twenty voice mail messages from Erica, trying to get him back to work. Trying to get him to care.

He erased all of them with one push of his finger.

But then the screen illuminated with a text message.

Twenty messages, you jerk. You've lost two clients. I've paid all the bills I can. Consider this my two weeks notice. Erica.

CHAPTER SIX

HE STARED HARD AT the words, trying to make sense of them. Erica was leaving. He searched himself for any emotional reaction, but felt nothing. It was as if it were someone else's incredibly prized personal assistant leaving.

That whole life, the office and the buildings, the door with his name on it, all of it seemed so far away. So removed from him.

The fact that he didn't care, not about losing Erica or his clients, actually terrified him.

Who am I becoming? he wondered.

His throat tight, he deleted the message only to have another one pop up that had been sent three hours after the previous one.

Okay. I've had a glass of wine and expensed a nice dinner on you. I realize leaving now would be a disaster. For you. You need help, Matt. Lots of help. Charlotte came by the office yesterday. She quit her job and is moving down to Houston with the kids to be with Jack. She says stop sending them money. She says they are fine. I believe her. I'm not quitting. Thanks for the steak.

Fine? He wondered. He tipped his head back and stared through the screen at a filmy white cloud passing over the moon. How is that possible? Charlotte had been an editor at the *Post-Gazette*—a job she'd loved, had worked so hard for. Jack used to brag about his wife, the mudraker.

Oh, God, he thought, struggling for breath. *Another life changed. Another life diminished by what I've done.*

With a shaking finger, he turned off his phone.

He rose, bathed in a pool of moonlight, the dark around its edges so black it seemed like the floor might end. Stepping out of the pool would mean a certain fall and he felt as though he'd been held in this spot for too long.

He was here, at the Manor, with these women day in and day out, waiting, but what the hell was he really doing for his father? Nothing. Being a handyman wasn't bringing justice to anyone. It was only giving him blisters.

The floor creaked over his head as they got ready for bed. He could talk to them about Vanessa, right now. Tell them about what people in town said about her, ask if it was true.

Don't hurt us.

He was reluctant down to his feet to hurt them, but he needed to do something, anything. Standing here in the dark, tallying the bloody mistakes he'd made would drive him out of his mind. Maybe he was halfway there—half mad with all of it already. It was the only explanation for what he was doing.

What he'd come to.

He forced himself to remember his father in his prison cell, sitting on the thin bunk owning it, holding court, like it was the high stakes room at the Bellagio. Just thinking about it was a gut punch. Seven years for a crime he hadn't committed alone.

Other people needed to be punished.

Unbidden, he remembered the girlfriend's graveyard eyes. The splotches of blood like ugly rust-colored flowers on her sequined gown.

The way she screamed and screamed and screamed when the ambulance took her boyfriend's body away.

He was here for justice.

And justice didn't care who got hurt.

With a cool head, he decided to look for a safe. Talking about Vanessa had gotten him exactly nowhere and bringing the town gossip into it wouldn't help.

The sounds of Katie's and Savannah's voices filtered down through the old floors and he knew he had to wait until the house was asleep before starting his hunt.

He turned on the camping light and picked up his sketchbook. He flipped past his sketches of the repairs and quickly went to work on a sketch of the interior of the house, which was basically two squares built on top of each other around a central courtyard.

On the first floor, he knew there was a living room and a kitchen and, considering the age of the house, he took a reasonable guess about plumbing and put a bathroom on the second floor above the kitchen.

An hour and a half later the house was silent, dark and heavy with the dreams of sleeping women. When he was sure he couldn't be caught, he began his search.

The old wood floors creaked, soft spots like rotten bruises on a peach under the rugs in the hallways. With every creak he winced and waited for the sound of Savannah's footsteps thundering down the stairs. They never came. Either she was sound asleep or the creaks weren't that loud.

He hadn't done any sneaking since he'd been a kid, and he felt ridiculously out of practice.

In the living room, where the cops had been that morning, he checked the walls. Running his hands under the paintings, he found nothing but plaster and spiderwebs.

He took a step into the center of the room, glancing

around for other places a safe might be concealed only to realize that all the paintings were of Margot at various ages and various stages of undress.

One, illuminated by a shaft of moonlight like a searchlight, was a young Margot, staring over her shoulder. She looked so much like Savannah it was eerie.

Forcing himself to turn away, to keep his mind on what he was here to do, he left the room.

Savannah's office only revealed a landslide of papers and enough computer equipment to launch a spaceship.

Research, he remembered from his investigator's reports, Savannah was a well-paid researcher.

Where does her money go? he wondered. Certainly not into the house. Savannah drove a nothing special car, wore nothing special clothes. No jewels, very little makeup.

Granted, Margot looked like a woman who demanded a certain amount of money for upkeep.

And, he thought, taxes on a house like this might be a pretty big chunk of change.

But still, it didn't seem to add up.

He wondered what she looked up on those computers while at the same time trying to convince himself that he truly didn't care. That knowing her, or wanting to know her any better, was in direct opposition to finding out the truth.

The drawers to her desk were open and filled with receipts and pens and about a hundred little Halloween packages of M&M's.

She has a sweet tooth, he thought, finding the idea utterly intimate as he stared down at the drawer as though it was stuffed with lingerie rather than months-old chocolates.

More than a little disgusted with himself, he left the office, shutting the door quietly behind him. At the end of the hallway were two closed doors, Margot's room and what he thought was the library. Both rooms had slices of light shining out under the doors.

The floor creaked behind him and he turned only to come face-to-face with a steely-eyed Savannah.

His stomach fell into his shoes.

"What are you doing?" she asked.

"I thought I heard something," he lied. The lie he'd planned and rehearsed. Some of the steel leached from her eyes and she licked her lips. He forced himself to be cold, to be numb to her. It was much harder than he expected.

"What?" she asked. "What did you hear?"

"Just some creaking. Old houses," he said with a shrug, trying hard not to look lower than her eyes—she was wearing that purple robe and its gleam in the moonlight was magnetic.

"Okay," she whispered, clearly torn, hesitant to leave him where he stood.

"You wanted me here," he reminded her. "To check things out at night, right?"

"Right," she agreed, and then repeated it. Stronger. "Of course. Thank you."

"You're welcome," he said and left first, feeling her eyes on his back as he walked away. She was suspicious, and he had to hope he found what he was looking for before she discovered the truth about him.

THE NEXT MORNING, Doug from the hardware store delivered the tiller and chain saw.

Matt met him by the curb and helped him unload.

"I'll take them around back for you," Doug said, his bland face alight with morbid curiosity.

"I got it," Matt said. His righteousness from last night had faded into a general unease, and bringing this guy into the Manor would only make him feel worse. "Thanks, though."

Doug peered over Matt's shoulder. "God, look at her," he said and Matt spun to see all the O'Neill women standing on the porch, glaring at him.

The only thing missing was a shotgun in Katie's hands.

"How did someone so beautiful get to be so mean?" Doug asked.

Something inside of him leaped, snarled, wanted to tear this guy apart for even looking at Savannah with that hate and ownership in his eyes, as though he knew everything there was to know about the woman.

Not your business, Matt. Stay out of it.

But the urge to protect the women behind him wouldn't go away.

"I swear she's the biggest bitch I've ever met."

"Well, women tend to get mean when people call them names," he said through clenched teeth.

Doug blinked at him, as if he didn't get it, and Matt waited for the words to sink in.

"Give it time, man, her true colors will come through."

That was the thing—Matt feared they already had. In those soft moments. The quiet ones. As she smoothed her daughter's hair away from her face. As she jumped over rocks. He thought of the M&M's, of her defiant eyes last night that didn't quite hide the worry she felt around him.

"You know, in my experience, men hate a beautiful woman for only one reason," Matt said.

"What's that?"

"The woman is too good for them and they know it."

Doug's eyes narrowed. "They're trash. Whores. Every

one of them, from the grandma on down. Why don't you ask Savannah who Katie's father is, huh?"

Matt reached out to curl his hand in the neck of Doug's shirt.

"There a problem here?" Margot's voice rang out like steel on steel behind him and he dropped his hand.

"Nope," Matt said, looking Doug square in the eye. "Doug was just leaving. Don't worry about delivering that sod," he said. "Give me a call and I'll come get it."

Doug grumbled, cast one more dark look over Matt's shoulder, and finally got back in his truck and drove away, a plume of dust behind him.

Matt released the brake on the tiller and picked up the chain saw before turning. Margot stood there, staring daggers at him as Savannah was stepping off the porch behind her.

"Don't say a word about Katie's father," Margot said, her face stony. "It's not something that gets talked about around here. Ever."

"Yeah," he said, wiping his neck with his shoulder, getting sick of the secrets. "There's a lot of that here."

Savannah came to stand next to Margot and lifted her hand to shield her eyes from the sun. "What's going on?" she asked.

Looking for the safe had gotten him nowhere. It was time to throw some cards on the table and see what these two had.

"According to Doug and his mother, the gossip around town is that some kid named Garrett is behind the break-in."

Savannah and Margot shared a loaded look. "That's what we thought," Savannah said. "Juliette is on it."

"He also said that Garrett is looking for a wall safe. Rumor has it you guys are hiding gems."

There was a long silent moment and Matt held his breath. *Come on,* he thought, *just give me something. One thing.*

Savannah laughed.

"Yes, termite damage and loads of gems. Makes perfect sense. Did Doug have anything else to say?"

Disheartened, frustrated, he shook his head and pushed the tiller toward the side of the house. He took a few steps before stopping.

He didn't want to be involved, but he couldn't help it. Doug's malice turned Matt's stomach, and he had to wonder how far such anger had gone.

He turned, looked Savannah in the eye. "Did Doug ever hurt you?"

Savannah's mouth fell open slightly before she pressed her lips into a white line. She shook her head, her eyes bleeding blue. "He's harmless."

Matt swallowed, clamped his teeth together and left before he did anything else.

THE NEXT MORNING, it was barely past dawn and he was sweaty and swarmed with bugs. Frustration ate at him, driving him to swing the scythe harder, faster.

No luck.

Four days. Four. Days.

Most of the kudzu was gone. The wall was totally repaired, a work of art, actually. He'd unearthed the bench and the broken fountain, and the rosebushes were trimmed to within an inch of their lives—he was an architect after all, not a damn gardener.

But that was it.

He'd searched every room except for Savannah's, Margot's and the library, which were all locked. This was so highly suspicious, he couldn't sleep at night thinking about all they might be hiding in those rooms.

But in the rest of the house, no safes.

Or, frankly, any sign of Vanessa.

Savannah was avoiding him like the plague and none of this brought him any closer to knowing where Vanessa or the gems were or why his father had been set up to rot in a jail cell alone.

As he attacked the vines, he became all too aware he had a pair of eyes on him from the cypress tree over his shoulder.

Not Savannah's—she watched him from the window of her office. And Margot stood sentinel at the kitchen window.

Katie watched him from the tree.

"Hi, Katie," he said, breaking the silence, his rhythm against the kudzu never slowing. "Whatcha doing?"

There was a long, slightly stunned silence and he grinned.

"I know you're there," he said. "No use pretending you're not."

An orange peel fell on his shoulder. He smiled and shrugged it off. It landed, a brilliant orange curl, in the pile of deep green weeds.

"I'm watching you," she finally said.

"Seems you should have better things to do."

Leaves rustled and there was a thunk as the girl dropped onto the cobblestones behind him.

"I don't."

"You bored?"

"Yeah."

"You want to help?" he asked, stopping long enough to glance over his shoulder.

She wore the top of her Asian red silk pajamas with

cutoff shorts, tennis shoes and sweat socks pulled up to her knees.

"No," she said and wrestled around in her back pocket only to pull out a deck of cards. "Want to play cards?"

He paused for a second then shook his head with a chuckle. Man, these O'Neills were never what he expected. "I'm working."

"Come on," she begged, her smile a glittery replica of her mother's in the surveillance picture he'd stared at far too long. It changed Katie's awkward features—the prominent nose, the messy hair and freckles—and he got a good solid glimpse of the beauty Katie O'Neill would be. "A card trick. Just one."

He couldn't say no to that smile, or to a bored kid. He remembered all too well what that was like, waiting in the car for hours on end while his father "worked" in some backroom card game. He set down the scythe and turned around, wiping off his hands.

"Let's see what you got," he said with a smile, expecting something along the lines of Go Fish.

With a flourish that would have made the old man proud, Katie shuffled and bridged, the cards a blur in her hands.

"You've done this before?" he asked, lifting his eyebrows.

"Watch the queen of hearts," she said, flashing him the old lady then breaking into a flimflam routine that would have worked on any corner in the city fifty years ago. "You watching?"

"Oh, I'm watching." But he was watching the nine of clubs, which had been next to the queen.

Katie gave him another glimpse of the queen then tucked her seamlessly behind the nine. "You see her?"

"I know exactly where she is."

Katie scoffed, her eyes bright, and fanned the cards, facing him with a flourish. "Pick her."

And he did, right away, tucked behind the nine. Katie's face fell. "You've got to work harder than that to fool me at cards. Don't hide the mark under the closest card. Pick a different card a few spots away." He took out the queen and moved her behind the three of spades, which was halfway across the deck.

"You play cards?" Katie asked.

"Some."

"Poker?"

He laughed, amazed at this little girl's capacity to surprise him. "I've played before."

Her ice-blue eyes narrowed. "You a shark?" she asked.

"What the hell do you think you're doing?" Another voice yelled and Matt and Katie turned to find Savannah bearing down on them from the doorway like a hurricane.

Katie pushed the cards into Matt's hands and he fumbled, dropping most of them.

"He was showing me card tricks, Mom," Katie said, blinking her blue eyes in an innocent act so bad Matt nearly groaned. But Savannah bought it. She grabbed her daughter and glared at Matt as if he were showing her how to play with matches.

"We don't play cards in this house," she said, her eyes ripping the skin off his body. She pushed her long blond hair off her face, away from her eyes and Matt realized she looked like a Valkyrie. A woman warrior out for blood. His.

What did I do? he wondered.

"Cards?" he muttered, like an idiot. According to his private investigator's reports hidden away in the sleeping porch, her brother, the middle one, had won the World Series of Poker last year. Her family not only played cards, they excelled at them.

"Not in this house," Savannah nearly hissed.

"I…ah…" Matt was struck dumb and Katie buried her face in her mother's neck, offering him no help at all. "I'm sorry?"

"Damn right you're sorry," Savannah snapped. "No cards. No tricks. No games."

He considered clearing his name and opening Savannah's eyes to the flimflam artist she was currently cradling against her chest like the last innocent on the planet.

But Katie lifted her head momentarily and shook it, fear in her eyes, and Matt didn't know if he was being conned or if she was truly scared. Either way, it wasn't much skin off his nose. One more lie added to his growing pile.

But he couldn't help wonder what scared Savannah so much about cards or gambling that she could lie to herself so completely, see the world so differently from how it really was.

He nodded, solemnly. "Got it. I am sorry. I was just passing the time."

"We hired you to work."

He arched his eyebrows in stunned silence. He'd been working his tail off and no one, not even an angry Savannah, could deny that. "Is there something wrong with the amount of work I've done?" he asked, his pride leaping. "Am I not doing enough?"

"No," she said, shaking her head. "I'm sorry. I'm… you're doing a great job."

Damn right he was. His hands were a bloody mess, his back felt broken at the end of the day and he had the sneaking suspicion he'd lost about five pounds.

Savannah seemed to chew her tongue for a moment, on the verge of saying something and he found himself hoping, even for a scolding. Four days of silence and now—with this fire in her eyes, her hands curling in the red hair of her rascal daughter—he found himself wanting her to stay. Wanting her around.

She was like a bright spark against a black sky.

Her eyes flickered over his face, he could almost feel them touch his lips and eyes. Breathing became difficult and his fingers twitched with a sudden wild impulse to touch her hair, a long straight piece of it that had fallen over her shoulder and glowed in the sunlight.

"Just don't teach my daughter any card games," she said.

Then the moment passed and she was gone.

Katie grinned and waved at him over her shoulder and his jaw nearly dropped.

Suckered. They'd all been suckered by Katie. He turned to pick up his tools, only to find Margot standing in the broken sunlight. A ghost in white linen and diamonds, holding a steaming mug of coffee. She carried a folded newspaper under her arm like she was a stockbroker off to the office.

"You're a shark," she said, her eyes sharper than a knife. "Aren't you?"

Matt shook his head, but Margot grinned anyway, a Mona Lisa curl to her lip that he couldn't read. He didn't know what any of this meant; he felt like he'd slipped down the rabbit hole.

"Come to my room," she said, making it sound like an imperial order. "Midnight tonight. We'll see whether you're a shark or not." She looked him up and down and turned, heading inside.

"IT'S LATE, KATIE," Savannah murmured into her daughter's hair, stroking it away from her young, damp face pressed into the bed pillow. "Do you want to go to sleep in my room again?"

Savannah half hoped her girl would say yes. Since the break-in, Katie had been bunking with her and it had been nice. More than nice, actually.

Katie's little body curled against hers in the darkness, her tiny feet pressed tight against Savannah's shins, had reminded her of when Katie had been a baby and they'd shared the same bed until her daughter had started to snore.

She still did, which was why Savannah only half hoped her daughter would want to go to Savannah's room.

"I want to sleep in my room," Katie murmured, reaching up to hold Savannah's hand. "Just stay until I fall asleep."

Savannah sighed and rolled over onto her back, staring at the ceiling, thinking of the burning of widows in India and the other extreme religious rituals she was getting paid to think about these days.

These thoughts only lasted a millisecond, superceded, as had been the case for far too long, by thoughts of Matt.

Matt in the hallway, his dark hair silvered by moonlight, checking out suspicious sounds. Which frankly seemed suspicious.

But then this morning, that thing with Doug.

She waffled between wondering how he was going to hurt them and how he was going to help them. Part of her resisted the notion that he was simply a good guy doing something decent for the O'Neill women.

She'd been taught not to trust by the best of them, so it was hard trusting Matt, who seemed so entirely trustworthy. Lord knows he was working hard enough.

The man worked through three shirts a day.

To her utter and total chagrin, she was counting. From her office window she was watching it all—the sweat that dripped down his neck, the way the sun hit his green eyes and turned them the color of bottle glass. How he used the bottom edge of his shirt to wipe his forehead, revealing a white slice of muscled abdomen.

She knew she'd overreacted to the card situation, but it had been such a shock after all these years to see cards being played at the Manor. They used to play all the time. But after Tyler left, he'd taken all the fun out of the place, and there'd been no cards. Then Katie had been born and Savannah had done everything she could to make sure the Notorious O'Neill garbage stayed in the past, or at least outside the walls of the house.

And Matt had brought it back in.

Like a draft through a cracked door, all sorts of things had come in with Matt Howe.

Desire was curling around her like a hot breeze, tighter and tighter until she couldn't think, couldn't breathe without wondering what that bead of sweat against his neck might taste like, what his hair would feel like between her fingers. His body, strong and—

"Mom?" Katie asked and Savannah turned to look at the little girl, startled and embarrassed by her thoughts. "Do you like Matt?"

"Do you?" she asked, hot with discomfort.

Katie shrugged. "I don't know."

"That's how I feel, too," she said and pressed her lips to Katie's forehead.

CHAPTER SEVEN

THE HOURS UNTIL MIDNIGHT crawled and Matt wondered, watching the clouds over the moon, what exactly Margot had in store for him.

Luckily, he wasn't conflicted about going. He was going—no doubt about it. This was his chance to get a look at the room, and better yet, to spend some time with Margot, see what he might be able to pry out of her.

And, the truth was, he was bored.

The dark hallways didn't so much as creak as he walked through them, avoiding the rotten spots he'd discovered. The dim light from under Margot's door guided him through the dark house.

At the door, unsure if he was about to be the object of a twisted Mrs. Robinson situation, he took a deep breath and knocked, the door creaking open slightly under his fist.

"Come in, my dear boy," Margot said, and he stepped the rest of the way in the room to find her sitting at a table, shuffling through a deck of cards. A cigar was smoking in a crystal ashtray at her elbow.

Behind her was nothing but shadows, the walls black blurs.

"Drink?" she asked, pointing to the tray of bottles on her dresser.

He shook his head. "What...ah—"

It didn't look like seduction, but he wasn't entirely sure of what it did look like.

"Poker," she said, the cards roaring as she shuffled them. "You're here to play poker." She quirked an eyebrow at him. "Perhaps you were thinking I brought you here for something else?"

He grinned, feeling a blush climb his cheeks. "Honestly, I didn't know what to expect."

"Five card," she said. "You can expect five card and as soon as—"

The door opened behind him and he nearly groaned, thinking he was about to be scolded by Savannah again, but it was Katie who came creeping in the door.

"She's asleep," Katie told her grandmother. "She snores."

"So do you," Margot said. Katie climbed up on a chair, setting three cookies on the corner of the table like thousand-dollar chips.

"Five card stud," Margot said, beginning to deal.

"Threes and nines wild," Katie added.

Margot stopped shuffling. "Aren't we past the training wheels?"

"One game with wild cards. Just one."

Margot sighed. "Fine. Threes and nines wild."

A long-standing, backroom poker game, he realized, taking in the slightly ridiculous sight of the eight-year-old girl and eighty-year-old woman, eyeing each other over their hands.

A small pile of cards grew in front of the empty seat and Margot paused, both of them turning to stare at him.

"You in?" Katie asked.

"Does your mother know you do this?" he asked Katie.

Katie and Margot laughed. "No way," Katie said.

"Savannah has strong feelings about gambling," Margot added.

"And drinking," Katie supplied.

"All things O'Neill," Margot said, lifting the cigar, the smoke curling across her face, obscuring her expression.

The hair lifted on the back of his neck. "Are there things about the O'Neills that warrant strong feelings?"

Like gem theft?

"Mom says we have to rise above our roots," Katie said.

"What are your roots?" he asked, his hands tapping a nervous tattoo against his pants leg.

"Sit down, boy," Margot said a smile as old as Eve on her face. "Maybe you'll find out."

Matt glanced between them, the aging mistress to musicians and politicians and the eight-year-old daughter of a woman he was growing increasingly fascinated by.

"What the hell," he muttered and sat down, picking up his cards.

"You *ARE* A SHARK," Margot cried an hour later, after he'd cleaned them out. Again.

"Yeah," Katie agreed, throwing the last of her chips at Matt, who ducked, laughing.

"I never said I didn't play cards," he said, raking the chips across the table. He'd played a lot of cards. More, probably, than any one man should, thanks to his father.

"Who taught you?" Margot asked, squinting at him through the smoke of her small cigar.

"My father," he answered honestly, stacking the chips without looking at the girls. The smell of cigar, the slick feel of the cards under his fingers, the stacks of blue chips in front of him, even the camaraderie of sitting with other players around a table, taking stock of each other all while pretending not to—it all coalesced into a bittersweet nostalgia. "He taught me how to play poker, tie a perfect Windsor and play Rachmaninoff."

"Sounds like an interesting childhood," Margot said, her voice quiet. He glanced at her and immediately regretted it. Card players and their all-too-knowing eyes.

"My father was an interesting man," he said, then realized he was beginning to dip into areas he had no business dipping into with these women. "But I haven't played since college. I worked for a civil engineer in the summer and the crew played almost every night. I made enough to pay for next year's tuition."

"You're not really a handyman, are you?" Margot asked, apparently determined to stray into those dangerous areas of conversation.

"I've been a lot of things. Right now I'm a handyman. You know," he said, changing the subject, glancing at Margot from under his lashes, "you're not so bad yourself."

An understatement—the woman was a player down to her toes.

"Thank you," she murmured graciously.

"You could head out to any casino and make enough to fix this place up."

She glared at him, all graciousness gone.

Oops, he thought.

"What's Rachmaninoff?" Katie asked, tucking her chin into her hand. "Is that another game?"

"He's a music composer," Matt answered quickly, thinking of those thunderous notes and the huge Russian drama of those concertos. "I used to play the piano."

"Piano!" Katie cried, perking up. "We—"

"Have you been in the library?" Margot asked, still watching like a wary old cat.

"I don't think so," he lied, knowing full well he hadn't been in the library. It was the other room with the light on under the door. Besides Savannah's bedroom, it was the last blank space on his drawing of the house.

"Next door," she said, easing away from the table.

"We're done?" Katie asked, stifling a yawn. Margot smiled, pushing back some of the girl's red hair.

"We are for tonight."

"Tomorrow?" Katie asked and Margot nodded her head toward Matt.

"Ask him."

He blinked, stunned.

"You gonna play with us again tomorrow night?"

This was the most comfortable he'd felt in six months, the most relaxed his mind had been. The ghosts were sleeping and he actually felt his bones, his muscles, everything was sinking back into him. His skin was his again.

Before he got too cozy with the aging and pint-size O'Neills, he reminded himself that it was about access. Margot was granting him more access.

"Sure," he said and stood. "The library?"

Margot tilted her head toward the room next door, but said nothing and stayed behind in her bedroom.

The hallway was silver with moonlight and as he opened the door to the library, the soft scent of dust and books and a hundred years of cigar smoking wafted out around him. A smell somehow as comforting as freshly cut wood.

Quickly he scanned the walls, running his hands along the shadows and under paintings, but he didn't find anything.

It took him a second to see what Margot wanted him to see. It was tucked back in the corner, hidden in darkness, but the corner of it caught moonlight and gleamed.

A Steinway baby grand. Black as night, slick as oil, and in his mood, totally irresistible.

He smiled, cracking his fingers as he walked over to it. He lifted the lid and pressed the slightly yellowed middle C, expecting the worst.

It rang out clear and in tune, echoing around the books and paintings.

He sat and closed his eyes for a second, remembering those lessons next to his father, and laid his fingers across the keys, Rachmaninoff coming back to him like a storm.

The music filled the room with lightning and he lost all sense of time until the door creaked open and Savannah stood there, staring at him as if he were a ghost.

"Oh—" he said and stopped, the music coming to a halt. "I'm so sorry. I—"

"Keep playing," she whispered. She stepped into the room, and through a shaft of moonlight he saw tears in her eyes. "Please."

Surprised, he nodded and finished the movement, trying hard not to stare at her as she stood there crying.

THE NOTES LINGERED, trailing across her skin like gossamer spiderwebs, and it was as if she'd been dipped backward in time. A pain, thick and clogging filled her throat and she was mortified to realize she was crying. Crying in front of Matt.

She stepped into the shadows and wiped her eyes, somehow full and drained at the same time.

He'd made this happen. Matt had called her from sleep and filled her with this sudden loneliness, this bittersweet pain, and she'd walked down here to feel more of it.

The long years she'd spent alone were suddenly too

heavy to carry and she sank into a wingback chair across the room from the piano.

"I'm rusty," he said after a long moment of silence. "But I've never made anyone cry before."

She laughed. At him. At herself.

"It's been a long time since anyone played the piano here." She sighed.

"That's a shame," he said. "It's a beautiful instrument." He ran the backs of his hands across the keys, the sound a musical zipper undoing her, note by note. "Do you play?"

She tilted her head back to smile at him. "Not well."

"Katie?"

"Sadly, Katie has no interest." She cleared her throat, all the words sticky. "My brother, Tyler, is the musician." She remembered those nights, after the shock wore off and the place began to feel like home. Tyler would play and Carter would sing and Savannah, young and happy and so blissfully unaware of the way her family would further splinter apart, would dance and dance and dance. "When Tyler left…" She shrugged and stared at the ceiling, wondering how to put all that pain into words. "Everything got quiet."

"I know that kind of quiet," he said, his voice low, and it was as if some lock deep inside Savannah got jimmied open and things she didn't like to feel came bubbling up— empathy, kinship, a certain understanding.

It was dangerous to feel this way in the moonlight, with this man. The two were a reckless combination.

"What happened?" she asked.

"My mom got cancer when I was eight, she left that kind of quiet when she died."

"I'm sorry," Savannah said, and his answering smile was ghostly in the moonlight.

"I'm sorry your brother left you." His fingers stroked the keys, making phantom sounds that pinged through her. "How long has he been gone?"

"Ten years." For ten years quiet had crept over this house until it felt like a tomb. And she was buried alive in it.

"Have you seen him?"

"Yes, but it's been a while. We went to Vegas once when Katie was little, but he hasn't come home since he left." She talked about it as if it wasn't hard. As if her family's absence wasn't an open wound on her heart.

"Do you have other family?"

"My oldest brother is in Baton Rouge. He's in city politics there and is trying to keep this part of his life quiet."

"This part?" Matt asked hitting a C sharp that reverberated through her body.

"The Notorious O'Neill part," she answered, keeping it vague. "Our colorful family."

"Ah, colorful family. I know what that's like."

"Your mother?"

He shook his head. "She was…" He paused. Sighed. "Blissfully, perfectly normal. A kindergarten teacher." He played a slow rendition of "The Wheels On the Bus." "She made dinner every night and sewed the holes in my clothes and washed my mouth out with soap when I swore. My father was the colorful one."

"They must have had an interesting relationship," Savannah said, happy to listen to him talk, to watch him in the shadows and moonlight. Her knight at rest. At ease.

Watching him eased her, too, and the loneliness lifted, the sadness evaporated.

"I think it was an interesting one-night stand." He grinned. "They weren't together when I was growing up. But to his credit, he took care of me when Mom died. He got me to school and taught me the piano—" He played something bright, a few notes of jazz and she wondered what other secrets their handyman kept.

"Do you have any brothers or sisters?"

"No," he said, the jazz coming to a slow stop. "But I grew up with a kid. Jack. He's as much a brother as I could ask for."

There was a whole lot of heartache going on behind those words and she nearly asked him where Jack was, or why thinking about Jack made him sad, but he cleared his throat and asked, "Where is your mother?"

The coziness surrounding them was split and she suddenly felt the evening cool in the room, the very late hour.

She wasn't going to answer—things had already gotten too far too fast with him. She could blame the music, but she wasn't going to answer that question.

"Savannah?"

She'd let the silence unfold until he got uncomfortable and stood and left. It's what she did whenever anyone asked about her mother—not that many people did anymore.

"I should go," he said and she heard him in the shadows, standing to leave and suddenly, she didn't want that. She didn't want to be alone. Not anymore. Not right now.

So, the words just fell out of her for the first time in years.

"My mom left us. Here. When my two brothers and I were just kids."

"That's—"

"A terrible story, I know. I lived it. I haven't seen her or heard from her in twenty years."

"Not a word?"

"No cards, no letters, no phone calls. Nothing."

Matt watched her, his eyes bright, focused. "You know she's alive?"

"As far as I know." The old bitterness welled up in her, coloring everything in bleak shades of gray and black. She put her hand to her chest, feeling the pounding of her heart.

"You have no idea where she is?" he asked and she shook her head.

As if he could read her, as if he knew her, he began the first part of "Für Elise," the music a balm, the notes winding around them, rebuilding their cocoon against the world. Thicker. Denser.

The music went on until it was just them, just this moment. She didn't want it to end.

She shifted, her robe sliding open across her legs, which gleamed white in the dim room. His fingers fumbled, hit a discordant note and the music jangled to an end.

Quickly, afire with something hot and wicked, she closed her robe, tucked her legs under her. She could feel him watching her, like sun on her skin, and she was thrilled and slightly unnerved by his attraction.

"Where's your father?" she asked, filling the silence with the first thing she thought of.

He said nothing, so she leaned around the edge of the chair to better see him, only to find him staring at her. Staring at her so hard it was as if he were trying to absorb her.

His eyes glittered in the darkness, touched with something wild. Something feral that called out to the buried wildness in her.

She couldn't breathe. Didn't want to if it would shatter this moment.

The longer he watched her, the hotter the fire building in the room became until she couldn't look away. She couldn't look away when he stood and walked to her chair as though he owned the room. The world. Never in her life had she seen someone so masculine he practically prowled. It made her feel small and feminine.

Womanly and damp.

He crossed the room, stepping through bars of shadow and moonlight, and she couldn't move. Couldn't say anything. Transfixed by the hard hot look in his eyes, her mind shut off.

He stopped in front of the chair, his pant leg brushing the edge of her robe. She should say something, ask him what he was doing. Be outraged or something. But she knew what he was doing and she wanted it.

A kiss. His lips against hers. His breath on her skin.

Bracing his hands against the back of her chair, he leaned over her. He smelled of cigars and whiskey and she wanted to eat the air around him he smelled so good.

"Jail," he said, his voice a purr. "My father is in jail."

She could barely follow his words, drunk as she was on the heat pouring from his skin.

"For…for what?"

"Theft." He leaned in closer, his eyes boring into hers. "He stole jewels seven years ago from a casino in Las Vegas."

He seemed to want a reaction from her and she couldn't begin to understand what that was. "I'm sorry," she whispered.

"Are you?" he asked, his eyes narrowed and she blinked, stunned, some of the hazy fog of lust lifting from her brain.

"Of course," she said. "That's terrible."

He stared at her a while longer then smiled, but she didn't believe it. There was something dark happening in

Matt and, like the glasses, it made him that much more attractive to her.

"It is terrible," he agreed, his eyes roving over her face and hair. The silence stretched out between them until she thought she might snap from the tension.

Kiss me, she thought. *Kiss me. Kiss me. Kiss me.*

"I should go," he whispered, pushing himself away from her. She nearly fell over, that's how far she'd been leaning toward him. Chills, hot and cold, crawled over her flesh.

Embarrassment made her sick to her stomach.

"Right," she said. "Me, too." Unable to look at him, fearing that he would see all those things she couldn't control, she stood and inched her way around him. Tightening the cinch on her robe, she contemplated the long cool hallway in front of her. Her cold and empty bed.

But then—gentle, barely there—he touched her elbow, her hair, his thumb against the corner of her lips.

She gasped with pleasure so acute, so sudden and sharp, she felt it like lightning through her body.

"You are so beautiful," he whispered.

Then he was gone. Out the door without a sound.

She remained where she was, alone and trying to breathe, trying to calm this sudden storm. But it didn't work and suddenly that side of her, the side she tried so hard to bury and ignore and pretend was not a part of her DNA, chimed in.

Go to him, the O'Neill in her whispered. *Just go to him. See if it's as good as you think it would be.*

She shook her head, as if trying to dislodge the curiosity, but rooted, it grew.

A kiss. Just a kiss. He's clearly inclined, would have probably done it himself if you weren't such a nun. A cold fish—

Her feet moved. They took her out of the room, down

the hallway, shutting up the voice before it got really mean. Her instincts drove her, compelled her, and she was at the door to the sleeping porch in seconds.

The doors, warped by years of humidity, didn't shut and she barely had to press on the etched glass to open them.

He stood with his back to her in a shaft of moonlight so dense it was if he stood in water up to his elbows. He ripped off his shirt, the movements violent, barely controlled. He was muttering something, swearing, but she didn't try to hear, distracted as she was by the dip in his spine, the flare of his back, the upper curve of his ass in loose, low-riding khakis. He was like a statue, strong and perfect, and she wanted to press herself against all that warm living flesh. The smooth skin and hard muscle.

He turned and rifled the shirt into the corner, the muscles in his abdomen shifting, flexing.

He stopped. Stopped moving, swearing, even breathing.

"Savannah?" he whispered, stepping through the moonlight to the darkness on her side. "You okay?"

Okay? she thought. Hardly. She was dying.

Her mouth opened as if to say, *just making sure you had enough blankets* or some nonsense, but she stopped herself. Her better sense, running the show for way too long, stepped aside and let the O'Neill take over.

She took a step toward him, glanced in his eyes to see if he shared this madness and saw the desire flare in their green depths. But he held up his hand as if to contradict all the heat between them and she didn't want that. Couldn't have it.

"Savannah, I'm not wh—"

She kissed him.

She kissed him to shut him up. To shut herself up. To feed the growing ache in her body.

It was awkward, off-kilter, her lips lopsided against his. She was actually kissing a good portion of his cheek.

Mortified but committed, she stood poised ready for rejection.

But it didn't come. His low growl fanned her flames and his arms curled low around her back and she was surrounded by his strength. His heat.

His lips, thick and full, were slightly chapped against hers, and the kiss was featherlight, a breath of sensation that roared through her like a flood on dry land.

It was chaste, innocent, but with a delicious promise of more.

He pulled her closer until she felt his heartbeat against her chest, his erection hard against her belly.

His tongue tasted the corner of her lips, fleeting and careful, as if beseeching entrance and she opened her mouth, letting him in.

It was so sweet, the slide of lips, the wet lick of tongues. His breath warmed her cheek.

Suddenly, it was more. The kiss grew rougher, his hands bolder. Her fingers pushed into his hair and held on to the coarse silk for dear life.

Her breasts rested against his hard chest and she arched, torturing herself with pressure. Nothing but silk between them and it was somehow hotter than if they'd been naked.

His hands roamed her back, sliding over silk to find the nape of her neck and he held her, owned her.

Savannah wanted to laugh. She wanted climb into his skin. She wanted this kiss to never ever end. Heat pooled between her legs and her breasts were so hot. So heavy. She ached without his touch there.

They kissed and kissed. A thousand kisses. Hotter and faster. Harder. His teeth raked her tongue and she slid her hands all over his bare skin, memorizing the muscles, flirting with the back waist of his pants.

And she could have done it forever, stayed locked in his arms for the rest of her life, but she could only go so far.

The past created a line in the sand and she would not cross it again, not with a man she didn't know very well, no matter what the moonlight did to them.

She pulled away. A kiss was as far as she could go, and as if they'd agreed on the boundaries Matt eased off, his fingers dragging over her hips slowly, milking the moment for all he could until they were no longer touching.

She panted, her lips cold, but she was grateful for his sensitivity.

His smile was wicked and sweet and she wanted to fall right back into him. But if she did, she knew down to her bones they would not stop. Not until her robe was gone and he was deep inside her.

His eyes flared, his hands fisted as if he knew it too.

"Good night, Matt," she said, her heart afloat in her chest. Her feet, as she went to her bedroom, hardly touched the ground.

HE HAD TO GO.

He watched her walk away, the most elegant, sensual woman he'd ever kissed and realized that leaving was his only option.

Too many lies. Too many secrets. There was no way he could explain himself, not after what had happened tonight. It would all seem like a lie. He'd come here trying to make one thing right and he'd only wreaked more havoc. Brought more pain.

He was a curse, a blight, and they were better off without him.

He pulled on his shirt, ripping the neck in his frustration.

Why had she followed him? It had taken every ounce of will to leave her in the library, but he'd done it because he knew it was right.

He was lying to her, for crying out loud. Using her for information, like a key to a lock, and as much as he'd wanted to kiss her in the library, he couldn't do it. Not after all the things she'd told him. The way she'd opened up, dropping all that chilly distance she'd been keeping between them.

But then she'd appeared in his doorway, practically trembling and he could no sooner turn her away than he could rip off his skin.

And God! *That kiss.*

So sweet and awkward. Innocent, practically.

Regret filled him with dirt and sand, weighing him down.

He tore at his hair and growled. What was he thinking, telling her about Jack? About his mom? He'd blame the piano for that.

Matt felt sick again. He would leave, and send them money. Not that it would repair what he'd done. Sending the girlfriend money wasn't going to change her lover's death, but he'd done that anyway.

It made him feel better. As though he was doing something. Fixing something. Anything.

He stepped toward the corner where he'd hidden his wallet and the files. All his truth, right there, steps away from where they'd kissed.

He wondered what it had cost her to come in here. How much of that formidable pride she'd had to swallow. To risk rejection. To press her perfect body against his and lay herself bare.

He picked up his wallet and the files, heavy in his hands

as if the information were weighted. Cannon balls he'd been using against the O'Neills.

What would she think if he vanished? He couldn't even stand to contemplate the baffled hurt in those blue eyes. It would be the ultimate rejection.

He sighed and stared at the moonlight through the glass roof.

He was a coward, a miserable liar, but he couldn't do that to her. He simply couldn't.

That left him with two options—more lies or the truth.

He took a deep breath and knew he couldn't tell any more lies.

He hated the person he was turning into, the man he was becoming.

He could fix this. Make it right.

Just the thought had him putting the files back under the pot.

Tomorrow, he told himself, he'd tell her the truth.

THE NEXT MORNING, Savannah wasn't fooling around. She perched on the counter and made herself a breakfast of hot coffee and cold sugar pie.

She'd barely slept last night, her body running hot and her mind concocting fabulous fantasies about Matt. Finally, she gave up the fight and decided to have some breakfast before the whole house woke up.

The early-morning sun was already hot, brightness shining in the window and C.J., uninhibited, rolled onto her back on the counter next to Savannah. Feeling benevolent, Savannah gave the old girl a good tummy rub.

She couldn't stop smiling.

Could not stop replaying that kiss in her mind. Her

lips still felt his. Her body was still warm as if from his touch.

It was hard actually, not to giggle. Not to wrap her arms around herself and laugh. She had a crush. An honest-to-God, real-life crush, and it was so much fun.

Exhilarating, to be honest, imagining what she would do when she saw him next. What he would say.

When they might kiss again.

Soon, she hoped. Very, very soon.

Good God, that man is something, she thought, scarfing down a big spoonful of pie right from the pan. Strong, generous, funny. Maybe she should give him a raise.

She laughed at the notion. Savannah O'Neill, Sugar Mama.

Tilting her head toward the sun, she hummed her favorite Van Morrison tune and wondered if fate or karma had brought Matt to her.

She was not in love—it took a lot more than music and a kiss to bring down the walls she'd put up—but, with a man like Matt, she knew she could be.

She laughed at the crazy thought, but it was undeniable. He was a good man, a valuable man of worth and honor.

Not at all like Eric.

It had been such a gamble sitting in that room with him last night, and that gamble had paid off in spades.

She felt light this morning. Full of hope.

See? she thought, chasing a rogue raisin around the pie dish. Indulging that O'Neill side of her, those…wilder instincts, didn't mean the end of the world. It didn't mean disaster. It could just be fun. She thought of her brother Tyler, who had wholly embraced all things O'Neill.

He had always been fun. The life of the party.

And for too long she'd thought fun was bad, because when it was over—and it was always over—it left her alone.

Her brother had left. Eric had left. Though he hadn't quite left her alone.

Enough, she thought, sick of being her own killjoy.

She'd kissed a man in the moonlight. Nothing bad was going to happen. No sky was going to fall down around her.

Maybe, she thought with a small smile, she could sneak into the sleeping porch and—

"You're an idiot."

Jumping at Juliette's voice, she whirled, pushing blond hair out of her way to find her best friend standing in the kitchen doorway.

"Juliette? What—"

"Tyler gave me a key a million years ago," she said, striding into the kitchen looking way too police chiefy for such an early-morning visit.

"It's not even 8:00 a.m.," Savannah said. "What are you doing here."

"Trying to prevent you from doing something stupid, but I think I'm too late."

Something cold, something awful slid into Savannah's joy.

She resisted it as hard as she could, threw up all kinds of walls and doors and locks. *Please,* she thought, trying to hug the memory of the night to herself. *Just let me have this.*

"Look at you," Juliette said, flinging a hand out at her. "Singing Van Morrison, looking like a cat that's found the cream and…Christ, that's sugar pie, isn't it?"

Savannah dropped the dish on the counter. "What's your point?" she asked, tugging the neckline of her robe higher.

"You slept with him, didn't you?"

"No, I did not." Savannah blinked, though somehow

what had happened last night felt more intimate than sex. "And even if I did, I'm a grown woman, Juliette. I appreciate your concern, but I don't need it. It's okay." She smiled, trying hard to hold on to her morning-after glow. It had been eight years—couldn't a woman kiss a handsome man without causing an uproar?

"It's *okay?*" Juliette asked, her hazel eyes wide. She shook her head. "Savannah, I hate to tell you this, but I got an e-mail from the FBI office in Baton Rouge, and that man—the man you clearly did something with, the man living here—is lying to you."

An icy shower of dread ran over her and the joy couldn't hold out. This was all too familiar. Why, she wondered distantly, the sugar pie turning sour in her stomach, did she have to make the same mistake twice?

"What are you saying?" she asked, as the cold seeped past her muscles and into her bones.

"Whoever that man is, he isn't Matt Howe. There is no Matt Howe."

CHAPTER EIGHT

"WHAT?" SHE ASKED, pushing herself down onto her feet, stumbling slightly because everything was suddenly numb. Cold.

Juliette reached out to grab her elbow but Savannah jerked away. She didn't want to be touched. Not now.

"What are you saying?"

"There are no Matt Howes who look like him who live in St. Louis. No birth certificates. No driver's licenses. No school records, hospital records. Nothing. That man is not Matt Howe."

But he was. She'd kissed him last night. She'd laughed with him. She put her head in her hands, reaching deep for a little strength. She'd told him her secrets.

"You're sure?" she asked.

"As sure as the FBI can be, and that's pretty damn sure."

Right. Okay. She licked her lips, struggling to figure out what to do right now. Offer Juliette coffee? Pretend like nothing happened? Pretend like her stomach hadn't been ripped right out of her?

Such. An. Idiot.

"You okay?" Juliette asked, more friend now than police chief. Savannah shook her head, not wanting pity or friendship or, frankly, anyone to witness this moment. This second brush with the bottom. "Did he hurt you?"

"Hurt me?" She laughed. No. The man had laughed

with her. He'd touched her, woken her up after the ice age she'd been sleeping in. "I told you, we didn't sleep together. We—" She couldn't admit they'd just kissed. Not when she couldn't explain how it had seemed like more...like an understanding, a beginning.

"Still, you're freaking me out a little," Juliette said, ducking her face to try and see into Savannah's eyes.

"Well, join the club." She took a deep breath and tried to think through the cloud that surrounded her. "Maybe this isn't a big deal," she said, hopefully, but Juliette's face was pitying. "Why does it have to be a big deal?"

"Men don't lie for no reason. He gave you a false name." She shrugged. "He's hiding something."

Which, of course, had been her suspicion from the very beginning. Then the bastard went and put on glasses and played the piano and put his hands on her weak and willing flesh and she forgot all those suspicions.

Finally, anger swept down like a flash flood and flushed away her numbness, the last lingering traces of her joy. A righteous rage that she would be taken for a fool—again— put steel in her legs and back and she stood straight, flinging her hair over her shoulder.

"What are you going to do?" Juliette asked, leaning against the counter. "You want me to take him to the station? Hold him for a few days?" She poured herself a cup of coffee.

"I don't need you breaking the law for me," Savannah said.

"All right. So? What are you going to do?"

Her body remembered the way he'd touched her. Her skin was permanently etched by his fingers. Her breasts and lips still tingled and ached. And it had all been a lie.

He'd slept in her house. In the same house as her daughter.

Good God. She'd caught him in the hallway a few nights ago. He'd said he was checking out a sound and she'd convinced herself not to be suspicious. Not to be dubious.

"I'm going to make him very sorry he came to my door."

"Atta girl," Juliette said as she picked up her ringing phone. "I'll wait around to see if we need to bury a body."

Savannah walked through the house, sure of her destination. Her course of action.

The old glass doors to the sleeping porch hadn't shut in years and she just slipped between them. A ghost. A wraith.

It was dark on the porch, the overgrown vines outside acting like shades against the sun. The white sheets on the bed glowed in the half-light, drawing her eye despite her intention not to look at Matt. His back rose like a mountain from the snowy sheets, beautiful, all that caramel skin over muscle and bone. His feet were bare and sticking out over the edge of the bed and it made him seem oddly vulnerable.

Good, she thought, hoping she'd find something that she could use to make him hurt. Hurt like she hurt.

The oddball lessons learned at Margot's feet resurfaced and her nimble fingers, always so much more silent and careful than her brothers' at such things, went through Matt's clothing, searching out clues, evidence, secrets.

Our little pickpocket, Tyler had called her a million years ago.

The remembered nickname brought back a gush of emotion she didn't want to feel. Not right now. Now, she wanted to be righteous and angry.

She'd put these strange skills behind her along with the gambling and card playing that her whole family loved.

That Matt had reduced her to this was one more thing to hate about him.

In the corner of his duffel bag she found his BlackBerry.

She scrolled through his e-mails, his phone contacts.

His name was Matt Woods. And he sure as hell wasn't a handyman.

She threw the phone back in the bag.

Matt's pockets were empty so she went around the room, a ghost on bare feet, finding hiding spots and hidden nooks.

She tipped over a broken dusty pot in the corner and found a black leather wallet.

And under that, a set of manila folders.

MATT DREAMED OF BOX HEDGES. And a pattern, a maze. Detailed and difficult, something a wild eight-year-old would get a kick out of. And at the center of that maze a secret heart. Lush bougainvillaea bushes, perhaps. Definitely some birds of paradise. A bench. A fountain, something old-fashioned and courtly that Margot would adore.

Someplace quiet for the sun to filter through Savannah's hair.

His eyes blinked open and in a heartbeat he knew what to do with the courtyard.

A maze. It was perfect.

Inspiration, gone for months, flooded back as if his taste buds were exploding at the mere scent of delicious food, only instead of food, it was Savannah who had inspired him.

Savannah in the moonlight. Savannah pressed against him, her lush curves lighting him on fire.

It was a new day, a fresh start.

The truth will set me free, he thought. *No more lies.*

There was something in him that glowed at the prospect.

A sound in the corner, something between a laugh and a sob, made him turn.

Savannah, pale as a ghost.

Holding his wallet.

Looking through his files.

His stomach bottomed out and he cursed.

"What…what is all of this?" she whispered.

He cleared his throat. The truth, he reminded himself, the pristine truth. He stood, not wanting to have this conversation naked, and yanked on some pants.

"Information I had gathered on you and your family."

"Information?" she whispered, paging through the pictures with shaking fingers until she came to the one of her and all that baffled hurt froze into anger.

"This is a nice one," she said bending back the folders. "It was Katie's last day of school. Where's her file?"

"I don't have one. My investigator didn't tell me about her."

"You just can't get good surveillance these days, can you?" Savannah snapped, her mouth trembling, but then she bit her lips. Her whole body was rigid, concrete and rebar.

He said nothing.

"Why?" she demanded. "Why would you pay a stranger to follow my family?" She flung out the picture of Tyler at a card table in Vegas, and another one of Margot in her car and the third one of her eldest brother, Carter, leaving his office.

Thank God she didn't get to the one of her mother.

She threw the rest of the files on the bed and took his wallet from the pocket of her robe.

"And why would you lie to us?" She quirked an eyebrow at him. "Matt Woods, is it?"

"I'll answer all your questions," he said, holding up his hands as if talking down a jumper. "But I need a few answers of my own."

"You!" she breathed, fury igniting her face. "You are in no position to ask any questions!" She hurled the wallet into the corner. "Get dressed. And get the hell out of here."

She whirled to leave but he got ahold of the sleeve of her robe. "Savannah, we need to talk."

"Talk?" she cried. She smacked at his hand and then, her mouth tight with fury and her eyes bright with tears, she slapped his face. So hard his head snapped sideways and his ears rang.

"You lied to me. To my family," she whispered. "Get. Out."

He shook off the sting of her blow and stared her down.

"I deserve that," he said and her eyes narrowed. "I deserve that and more and I'm truly sorry for lying to you. But you never would have talked to me if I didn't do it this way. My name is Matt Woods. Howe was my mother's maiden name. I need—"

"You need to leave, Matt." She spat his name like it was rotten meat.

He felt like shit. This was a total nightmare and not at all how he imagined things going. But he'd come here for a reason and he wasn't going to leave without getting some answers of his own. Savannah might not know where her mother was, but there was still the small matter of the gems to be considered.

"Not until I have a chance to explain and get some answers."

"You have got to be kidding me," she said. "Like I'm going to answer any of your questions." Her anger cracked and sadness leaked into her face, her voice. The way she held herself, as though she was losing more strength with each passing second, made him want to howl. "Just go. I don't care what you have to say."

Anger, he could handle, but this sadness gutted him.

He shouldn't have done this.

Don't hurt us.

Remembering her words sliced at him, tore him to ribbons.

He was trying to fix things and he'd only made them worse.

"Wait a second." Margot's voice cut across the porch like a knife. Right. It wasn't only Savannah he'd lied to, and Margot didn't seem sad at all. Her face was utterly composed, her eyes snapping. She was furious. "You might not care, Savannah, but I sure as hell do."

"What's going on?" Katie asked from her spot at Margot's side, and he blew out a hard breath as he smashed, face-first, into rock bottom. He'd lied to a kid. A kid. Tried to use a kid for information. *Christ, what is wrong with me?* "Why doesn't Matt have any clothes on?"

"An excellent question," Margot said, her voice tart and Matt saw Savannah stiffen, her lips go white. He stepped in front of her, shielding her from Margot's chilling stare.

Margot blinked, surprised. Frankly, so was he, but he'd hurt Savannah enough. He wouldn't let anyone throw around words to hurt her more.

"Interesting," Margot said, watching all of them. "Why don't you get dressed, Matt, and meet us all in the library in ten minutes."

"I have some questions of my own," he told her, meeting

her flinty blue eyes. "And I'm not leaving without some answers."

"The library," Margot said. "And let's make it five."

SAVANNAH STOOD outside the library doors and forced herself not to twitch. Not to chew on her nails. Her palm still stung from the slap, her face still burned from a sick shame, but she forced herself to be the eye in the middle of the storm.

Utterly and totally still. Composed. Even though she seethed.

He was in there. Sitting at the piano.

Wearing those damn freaking glasses!

Her head hit the wall with a quiet thunk.

"Slightly overdressed, aren't you?" Margot's voice accompanied a hand at her shoulder and Savannah shrugged it away.

Just as she tried to shrug away memories of his hands and lips, his kiss.

"I'm cold," she said, pulling the edges of her cardigan around her waist. A cardigan over a turtleneck was overkill for summer in Bonne Terre, but there was no way she was showing that man an inch of her flesh.

"Your hair—" Margot reached up to touch the tight bun at the back of Savannah's neck but Savannah stepped away.

"It's fine. Everything is fine. Let's get this done with."

Savannah stepped toward the door, ready to face down the devil if it meant Matt whatever-his-name-was would be leaving, but Margot put a hand on her shoulder.

"You want to tell me what happened?" Margot asked.

"No." She laughed. "I definitely do not."

"You slept with him."

"Who do you think I am?" she asked. "Juliette asked me the same thing and no, I did not sleep with him."

"You like him."

Savannah snorted. "Liked, maybe."

"After Eric— Don't glare at me, Savannah."

"I don't want to talk about this, Margot."

"You never want to talk about this," Margot snapped.

"Lower your voice, for crying out loud."

"You didn't want to talk about Katie's father when it was happening, or when he left, or when you got pregnant or—"

"Mom?"

Savannah whirled to find both Katie and Matt standing in the doorway.

"Honey?" The word sounded like a croak. Savannah hoped the expression on her face was a smile, she wanted it to be, but judging by Katie's confusion and Matt's horror, she wasn't quite hitting the mark.

"What are you talking about?" Katie asked, her voice so small, her eyes so worried as they darted between Margot and Savannah.

Savannah glared hard at Margot. This wasn't something they talked about. Ever. Katie had never even heard the name Eric.

"Mom?"

"Ah—" Her mind was a wilderness, nothing but bears and dark and fear. Lots of fear. She didn't want to cry, or scream, or slap the glasses off Matt's handsome face, but she felt dangerously close to all three.

At some point this conversation was inevitable, she understood that. She wasn't stupid. But in the few times she'd been brave enough to imagine a scenario, Katie was older, Savannah was more prepared and it didn't take place in front of another man who'd lied to her.

When her world fell apart, it really fell apart.

"Me," Matt said, quietly, his eyes dark and serious behind his glasses. "They're talking about me."

Katie's gaze darted to him, fury sending out sparks.

Savannah didn't—couldn't—say anything. Looking at him, at his sympathetic eyes, she had no words. He had proven he was no knight in shining armor, he no longer needed to act the part.

Regardless, he'd given her a way out of this much-dreaded conversation.

Perhaps she'd thank him by not smacking him blind.

"Why don't you go play games on my laptop," Savannah said to Katie—a rare treat the girl would never be able to resist.

"Okay," she said warily, knowing something was up.

"Go on," Savannah urged. "It's in my room. I'll come up and play with you in a few minutes."

They all watched Katie climb the steps.

"We should go inside," Margot said, as if inviting everyone to tea.

"Absolutely," Savannah said and stormed past Matt, determined not to smell him or feel his heat.

Juliette stood inside, milky sunshine splashed across her face as she stared down at a framed photo in her hand, picked up from the table chock-full of family pictures.

"What are you looking at?" Margot asked.

"Nothing," Juliette said quickly, practically throwing the picture back on the table. "Old pictures." She turned with a bright smile. "Are we ready for the lynching?"

But Savannah didn't believe that smile for a moment, because it was Tyler grinning up from that photo, looking wild and handsome and totally capable of breaking a young Juliette's heart.

However, the moment didn't have room for Juliette's

old pain—it was practically bleeding with recent hurt. Savannah could feel everyone behind her, watching her, and she hardened her heart, surrounded it in glass and cement and buried everything she felt about last night and Matt as deep inside of herself as she could.

When she was blank and cool and detached she turned and pinned Matt to the wall with her gaze. He appeared startled for a moment, as if he hadn't expected her to fight, but then his own face got hard, his eyes cold. The handyman vanished. The musician, the man she kissed were all gone.

Someone she wasn't the slightest bit attracted to stared back at her.

Good, she thought.

She was ready for a fight.

"Why don't you tell us who you really are and what you're doing here?" she asked, pleased with her icy tone.

"My name isMatt Woods and I'm an architect in St. Louis."

The truth felt like being punched in the gut, but Savannah didn't even flinch. She watched him, hating him.

Juliette made a big show of writing everything down.

"I'm not lying," Matt said, eyebrow raised.

"Then you have nothing to worry about," Juliette said, tucking her pad and pen back in her pocket.

"Why are you here?" Savannah asked, biting out every word. "Why are you investigating us?"

"My father is Joel Woods."

"Who?" Margot asked, sitting in the wing chair Savannah had sat in last night. Matt's head snapped around.

"Does that name mean something to you?" he asked.

"No," Margot said with an indifferent shrug. Savannah almost smiled—no one did indifferent like Margot.

"You're sure?" he asked, his eyes like lasers under his glasses.

"Why would it?" Margot asked.

"What about The Pacific Diamond? Ring any bells? Or the Ruby?"

"Sounds lovely, but I have no idea what you're talking about," Margot said, blinking up at him.

He took a deep breath, turning to face Savannah. She wanted to curl up into a little ball so that not even his gaze could touch her, but she squared her shoulders and stuck out her chin.

She could practically hear Margot applauding.

"Last night," he said, and Savannah shot him a shut-the-hell-up look, which he ignored, "I told you the truth about my father. Seven years ago, he was arrested for stealing a priceless set of jewels called The Pacific Diamond, Emerald and Ruby from an ancient gemstones exhibit at the Bellagio. At some point during the drop-off, two of the jewels were stolen from my father. He was caught with the emerald but the diamond and the ruby are still missing."

"I still don't understand what that has to do with us," Savannah said.

"That was my father's first job—he wasn't a thief by trade and I don't think he was a very good one. His partner, who had some experience, hired my father for his knowledge of the casino. But when they went to the arranged meeting place to exchange the jewels for their fee, three things happened. The ruby and the diamond were stolen from my father, the cops showed up..." He hesitated.

"And?"

Matt licked his lips. "Your mother was there."

Blood roared through her and she leaned against the wall because she was suddenly light-headed. She couldn't feel her hands or feet, but her heart was scoured, bleeding acid.

This was about her mother? He was here because of

her *mother?* Last night— She couldn't even finish the thought. Bile churned in her stomach and her throat ached with unvoiced screams.

"That's why you kept asking about her?" she breathed.

"I thought you—" He shook his head. "It doesn't matter anymore. I was wrong and I'm sorry, Savannah."

"You thought what, exactly?" she spat, probing to see how far his betrayal went.

"I had reason to believe she might come here."

"Never. She would never come here."

"And then when I got here you wanted security cameras in your garden and people kept breaking in, clearly searching for something."

"So?"

"So." He nearly laughed. "That's not normal, Savannah. It seemed like you two were hiding something. Something of value."

He turned to Margot. "Is there any chance that Vanessa might have stolen the gems then hidden them here?"

"No," Savannah said.

"But with the break-ins—"

"I would know if my mother was here!" she cried, then sucked in a deep breath, feeling totally out of control. "Or if there were gems hidden in my house."

Margot nodded in agreement.

"Savannah, please," he whispered, "understand, I think that there—"

"Get out," she snapped, thrusting her finger toward the door. "We don't know where my mother is and we certainly—" she laughed because it was ludicrous and frankly it was either laugh or scream "—don't know anything about your father and stolen gems."

"I'll leave," he said. "I will, I just want to apologize."

"We heard you," she said. "Now go."

"Wait a second," Juliette said, stepping into the heated air between them. "You said your father was arrested seven years ago. If Vanessa was at the drop-off seven years ago, why are you here now? Not then?"

"My father just told me the truth about having a partner and…Vanessa's involvement in the theft. He'd been taking the blame himself for seven years."

Savannah reached the end of her rope. "Who the hell cares?" she cried. "No offense, Juliette, but the particulars don't matter." She stalked up to Matt, getting as close as she could stomach. "I don't want you here."

"You should know, Savannah." His eyes were sad, careful, and suddenly she knew she needed to brace herself. "Your mother has been in New Orleans most of the past five years."

Savannah swayed on numb legs and looked to Margot, who sat cold and still as a statue. "Did you know that?" she whispered.

Margot shook her head.

What did it matter, she wondered, hysteria buzzing along her nerve endings. New Orleans? The Moon? Six feet underground? Her mother was gone to her.

But somehow, as much as she wished it didn't matter, it did. That Vanessa was only a few hundred miles away stung like salt in an old wound.

"I'm sorry, Savannah," he whispered. "I know—"

"You don't know anything." She suddenly turned and left because she couldn't stand to look at him any longer.

Pulling back her hair, wearing her sternest clothes, surrounding her heart in cement—none of it worked. She was broken. Hurt. And all she wanted was him gone.

CHAPTER NINE

MATT WATCHED Savannah leave with his gut in his shoes. She was a different woman this morning. Cold and hard, worse even than the prison warden. She was an ice queen, the warm vibrant woman who'd laughed and kissed with him last night miles underneath her frigid exterior.

You did this, he told himself. *Because you were so stupidly hell-bent on your own course you didn't see the truth, just like you were with Jack and the buildings in St. Louis.*

Just like he always was.

What is wrong with me? he wondered, staring blindly out the door. *What is missing in me that I can't see the pain I cause?* ·

That he'd hurt Savannah, adding her name to his list of people he'd managed to wound in his own blindness, was an ache in his chest.

If he could pull off his skin, rip out his memories, he'd do it. He'd pay in his own blood for the hurt he'd caused everyone he touched.

He wished he could change the last twenty-four hours.

"I didn't mean to hurt her," he whispered, knowing Savannah's two guard dogs were hungry for his flesh.

"Sure," Juliette said, her sarcasm like being raked over hot coals. "Because women love it when you lie to them and then sleep with them."

"We didn't sleep together."

"Well, you did something," she said. Juliette stalked toward him, every inch of her a police chief. Her hands on her waist—inches, he noticed, from her gun. "Do as she says," Juliette whispered, her green eyes like steel. "Leave before you bring any more trouble to this house."

Then she was gone, leaving him alone with Margot. His comrade from last night's poker game was nowhere to be found. Instead she watched him, steely-eyed and unreadable.

There was no point in trying to justify himself to these women. He'd done so much damage, was in a hole so deep, there was no getting out.

He could only leave—this house, these women. Savannah.

"I'll pack and be gone in an hour." He wasn't three steps before Margot stopped him.

"I would like those files," she said, holding out her hand. Matt didn't see any reason not to give them to her, other than his sick desire to keep that photo of Savannah for himself, a talisman against the lonely, ghost-ridden days ahead.

He put the files in Margot's elegant hand and she flipped through them, her face betraying nothing.

"I assume you investigated your father's partner with the same thoroughness?" she asked, tucking the files under her arm.

"My investigator couldn't find any trace of him. Anywhere. He's vanished."

"His name?" There was no sign of the Southern flower in Margot at the moment. She was all business. Cold business.

"Richard Bonavie."

She nodded sharply, her lips white at the edges. "Do you know his relationship to Vanessa?"

Matt nodded. They'd been married, Richard and Vanessa. And now, judging by Margot's reaction, his suspicions were dead-on. "Richard Bonavie is Savannah's father."

"I assume you will keep that information to yourself," Margot said.

"I'm leaving," he said, "I don't see how it—"

"I hired you to do a job," she said and his jaw dropped.

"You want me to stay?" he asked. "You can't be serious."

Margot stood and approached him, her gambler's eyes taking him apart piece by piece. "We gave you a deposit on your work."

"I haven't cashed the check," he told her. The last thing he was going to do was take their money. "I was never going to. I'll tear it up and pay you more, give you a bigger budget. I can send a crew down here and you'll have a back courtyard that magazines will be calling you about."

She shook her head. "We don't want more people here," she said. "And I'm quite sure Savannah wouldn't want your money."

"Well, she certainly doesn't want me here, either."

"She did last night."

Matt gaped, feeling like a teenager caught with his pants down.

"Stop acting like a virgin," Margot said. "You're here, you've been paid and there's still work to do. You'll stay until it's done."

He shook his head. "This is not a good idea."

"You're going back on your word?" she asked, making it seem like going back on his word was somehow worse than what he'd done.

Savannah, he thought, the pain he'd caused her echoing through all the empty and rotted spaces in him.

"You can make this right," Margot said, sympathy shading her voice.

"You don't know me," he whispered, eroded and crumbling. "Everything I touch these days breaks."

Margot took a deep breath and patted his arm. "Savannah's tough," she said. "Now get to work."

SAVANNAH REFUSED, absolutely refused, to lie in bed, staring at the old lace canopy of her four-poster bed like some heartbroken heroine in a movie.

I should get a new bed, she thought. The overblown princess bed that had been her dream come true as a child was ridiculously irrelevant.

She told herself she kept it—the bed and the canopy and the lace and the pillows—for her daughter, but she was the one curled up here at night.

A lonely princess.

What garbage, she thought, furious with herself for getting maudlin.

Since Katie was no longer in Savannah's bedroom—no doubt having gone on some eavesdropping mission—Savannah decided to get some work done.

She kicked aside one of the gazillion useless little pillows she loved so much and dug out her laptop.

She pulled up all the files on religious mutilation in Indonesia.

Castration. She would do some work on male castration.

"Mom?"

Savannah turned toward her daughter, who stood in the doorway in bright red rain boots, the silver chopsticks

Margot brought back from her cruise pushed willy-nilly through her hair.

"I brought you something to eat," she said, stepping into the room and heading right for the bed with a plate of food.

The plate had all of Katie's favorites—Margot's pralines, barbecue potato chips and an apple next to a pile of peanut butter.

"Thank you, sweetie," Savannah said, making room for her daughter. "How are we going to get that peanut butter on the apple?"

Katie picked up the bright red fruit and rolled it in the peanut butter.

Savannah laughed so hard tears burned her eyes.

"Thank you," she whispered when Katie handed her the messy apple. She wasn't hungry, but she didn't have the heart to tell Katie that.

"Hey, Mom? Who is Matt?"

Savannah's numb fingers couldn't hold the fruit and it fell to the floor with a thunk, peanut butter everywhere.

"I honestly don't know," she said. "He lied to us."

"Did you know him before?"

"Before?" she asked, looking down at her daughter. "Before what?"

"Did you have sex?"

Savannah choked.

"You told me about sex, Mom."

"I know," she said. She'd told her daughter about death, drugs, Republicans, homosexuality and where babies come from. Just not where she'd come from. "But I don't think I want to talk about my sex life with you."

"But you had sex with that Matt guy?"

"Why are you asking me this?" she barked, and immediately regretted it. Katie stared down at her fingers, put back a praline and sighed.

"I'm sorry," Savannah said. "It's been a weird morning."

"Is Matt leaving?" Katie asked, and Savannah was grateful for an eight-year-old's attention span.

She'd never claimed to be a very good single mother.

"Yes," she said, feeling a door slam shut. No more sweat-soaked shirts in her back courtyard. No more green eyes watching her. No more thundering, soul-pounding music making its way up the stairs to her room. No more kisses in the moonlight. No fun. No recklessness. No more O'Neill inclinations running amuck.

No more Matt Howe. Or Woods. Whatever.

No more Matt.

She lifted her neck, swallowing against the phantom sensation of a collar around her throat. Tears burned behind her eyes for no good reason.

"Are you going to cry?" Katie asked.

"Absolutely not."

"Good." Katie grabbed a praline. "We don't need him here."

"You're absolutely right," Savannah said, willing herself to believe it. She pulled her daughter close, tired from a night of weaving fantasies around a man who did not exist. A nap was what she needed, she decided, closing her eyes against the world. Maybe she'd sleep the day away and not have to watch him leave.

"We don't need anyone else," Katie whispered and Savannah gave her a squeeze in agreement.

A FEW HOURS LATER, Savannah woke to sunshine on her face and the snick and slash of Matt's scythe through the vines of the back courtyard.

She pushed her face deeper into her pillow, her heart finding a quiet rhythm alongside Matt's work.

Snick. Snick.

Snick. Snick.

It was a nice way to wake up. Calm. Comforting. Totally—

Wrong.

She sat up, flipping her hair out of her face. Pillows slid to the floor as bright white fury filled her heart.

Unless it was Margot herself out there doing manual labor, she was dead. *Dead.*

Flying down the stairs, her feet barely touched the treads. She swung her hair into a knot on her head, ready to do battle. This morning had been emotional, no doubt about it, but it had been settled.

Matt was supposed to be gone.

Sunshine blinded her when she threw open the doors to the courtyard and she nearly tripped over her daughter, who sat on the step.

"Hey, Mom. I thought he was leaving."

"Hi, Katie," she said, pressing a quick hard kiss to the top of her head. "He is, don't worry. Where is he?"

"Back there," she said, pointing to the wild area past the cypress.

"Go on inside," Savannah said, wanting to ensure her daughter couldn't be called as a witness when Savannah was brought to trial for murder.

"No way, Mom." Katie shook her head.

"Go," Savannah said, giving her a hard look until Katie sighed dramatically and finally left.

Savannah flew into the bush.

"What the hell are you still doing—"

Sweat ran down his back. His very naked back. Suddenly Savannah felt every degree of the midday heat.

"Here," she finished, trying to end strong. Trying to keep her eyes off his smooth skin.

He turned, dropping the scythe and wiping an arm across his brow. "Working," he said, his eyes totally empty. "I'm going to finish what I started."

"It's not necessary," she insisted.

"Trust me, it is," he answered, and she got the sense he was talking about something else.

Not that I care, she reminded herself. *Not that it matters one bit.*

"You've been fired."

"Talk to your grandmother.'" He blinked for a moment, and his dead eyes flared with life. "I am sorry," he said. "I never meant to hurt anyone."

"Well," she snapped, hating that he knew he hurt her, "it's what happens when you lie to people."

She left quickly, relieved that her battle lay with Margot.

Margot was stretched out across her bed, Matt's files around her and Katie tucked up beside her.

"Did you know your brother Carter has been promoted to Mayor Pro Tempore of Baton Rouge? He's the president of city council." Margot put down the files and beamed, the proud relative. "Isn't that incredible? So smart, that boy. I always knew—"

"It would be incredible if he picked up the phone and called to tell us himself," Savannah barked, feeling raw and pissed.

"Well, I imagine he's busy," Margot said. "Chief of—"

"Why is he still here?" Savannah demanded, unwilling to be sidetracked.

"I can only assume you are talking about Matt." Margot put down Carter's file and took off her reading glasses.

"I want him gone."

"He's not leaving."

Savannah blinked, speechless, stunned by Margot's insensitivity.

"He lied to us, Margot. He had us investigated."

"With due cause, I think. He was trying to get justice for his father. It's pretty noble, once you think about it."

"*Noble?* His father's a thief and Matt is a fraud!"

"He was a fraud. And now, we have a very contrite handyman."

Savannah could only gape.

"Shove over." Margot gave Katie a jostle and Katie scrambled to make room. "Come sit down," Margot invited, patting the bed right beside the picture of laughing Savannah.

"Tell me you're joking," Savannah said through numb lips.

Margot shook her head. "We need the work done."

"We'll get someone else."

"We tried that already," Margot said, stretching out her legs.

"I don't want him in my home."

"I'm not dead yet, honey," Margot said, a hundred percent resolved, and a resolved Margot was an unshakeable one. "So it's still my house."

Savannah felt betrayed down to her toes. She finally sat on the corner of the bed, defeated and tired. "What are you doing?"

Margot reached out to touch her hair. "You liked him, honey," she whispered as if he were a puppy in a window.

Savannah shook off the touch, horrified. "You're matchmaking?"

Margot shrugged and winked at Katie, who was watching the exchange like a starved dog watched a chicken bone.

Savannah, overcome on all sides, fell backward on the bed.

"Come on, honey," Margot said. "It's only a few days and we really do need to get that work finished. And considering his guilt and his profession, I think it's safe to say we're going to get far more than we paid for."

We already did, Savannah thought, her unruly flesh tingling.

"Mom doesn't want him here," Katie said, the little pit bull, and Savannah squeezed her leg.

"It's fine." Savannah sighed. "But I'm having nothing to do with him."

"Sure you are," Margot said, her voice rich with a feminine knowledge that put Savannah's teeth on edge.

"I'm not."

"I heard you."

"Who's this?" Katie asked, picking up one of the files. She twisted it so Savannah could see the photo.

Savannah's blood momentarily stopped in her veins.

Mom.

The beauty in the picture was the mother she hadn't seen in twenty years.

It was Vanessa as Savannah remembered her, getting into a car. Her eyes hidden behind glasses, her hand lifted in a merry wave that seemed to say, "I'll only be gone a few minutes."

A lie, that gesture.

"Your grandmother," Margot said, when Savannah couldn't seem to find the words.

"How come she's not here?" Katie asked in the simple way of kids. "And why don't Uncle Tyler and Uncle

Carter come visit?" Katie pulled up pictures of Carter and Tyler.

All of the reasons seemed lame. Stupid. Years seemed to go by so fast.

"I'm going to make sure Carter and Tyler come home for Christmas," Savannah said. "It's time."

"That would be lovely," Margot said. "But we'd have more luck if we accepted Carter's invitation to spend the holiday in Baton Rouge. You know he doesn't like his past getting mixed up with his present."

"I don't think coming home for one Christmas is going to kill his professional career," Savannah snapped.

Margot eyed her. "It also wouldn't kill you to leave Bonne Terre."

"*I'd* like to go to Baton Rouge," Katie said, her eyes bright with the prospect. Katie hadn't been out of the parish since she was a year and a half and Tyler had paid for tickets for the two of them to go to Vegas. Baton Rouge was like going to Mars.

"They can come here," Savannah said, closed up tight against the idea of going to them, the deserters. "This is their home."

Margot shook her head. "Not to them, it isn't." Savannah didn't say anything. She knew what Margot was trying to do, but this was their home, Savannah, Tyler and Carter's. The home they made after Mom left them here. The home that kept them safe, protected. Together.

Until they left it.

"I don't understand why you take it as a personal betrayal that they left." Margot sighed. "Or why you think this house will fall down if you go. I asked you to come to Las Vegas last year. And last month, in the Far East, Anthony would have been delighted to have you—"

"Right, I'm going on a trip with you and your boy-friend."

"Just friend, honey." Margot smoothed back white hair from her forehead. "Boyfriends are for children."

This conversation was slipping from uncomfortable to ridiculous.

"I have to get some work done," Savannah said and stood, freeing herself. Margot had been obsessed lately with Savannah's lack of travel. Like she should take off every few months for foreign lands the way Margot did.

She wasn't that kind of person. Foreign lands were not for her.

"Honey?" Margot asked. "You don't suppose Matt was right, do you?"

"About what?"

"About Vanessa hiding the gems here?"

Savannah swung incredulous eyes to her grandmother. "Do you?"

Margot pursed her lips. "I guess not."

"There are no gems in this house." Savannah laughed. "Please. We would know. I would know. How would she get in and out without me knowing it?"

"But the break-ins?"

"High schoolers," Savannah said. "Just like it's always been."

MATT HEAVED down another square of sod, lining up the edges.

Don't. Think.

Don't. Think.

Bugs swarmed. Sun burned.

Don't. Think.

Not about his father.

Not about Jack.

The accident.

Savannah in the moonlight.

Don't. Think.

His world was reduced to the stretch and pull of his muscles, the river of sweat down his back.

He didn't look up. Didn't stop.

The files were gone, his obsession over his father's setup deflated with one sharp, wounded look from Savannah.

I can fix it.

What a joke. He couldn't fix anything. Shouldn't even try.

Something orange was flung into his eyes and he looked up to see Katie scowling at him from a low tree branch. She lifted her hand and hurled the peeled orange at his chest.

The fruit was right on target and the juice and pulp exploded against his body, up into his eyes.

"We don't want you here!" she cried, then vanished in the leaves, leaving nothing but silence and the smell of orange in the air.

Suddenly, there was a roar in his head. The girlfriend, Savannah, his father and Jack, all screaming for attention, all wanting to divide him into parcels of pain. Of regret.

Until there was nothing left of him.

He would finish this, then the ghosts could have him.

CHAPTER TEN

"Wow, LOOK AT THAT new greenhouse. It's gorgeous. Seriously, your courtyard looks like a magazine spread," Juliette said, sitting on Savannah's printer table so she could stare out the window at Matt. "That guy doesn't stop, does he?"

"Who?" Savannah asked, pretending to be distracted as she saved files and sent e-mails. Done. Her work for Discovery was done.

"Like you don't know," Juliette said, grinning. She leaned over and reached into Savannah's bottom drawer for the Halloween candy she kept there.

"I don't," she said, knowing she sounded like some kind of spinster librarian. Which she was. And she was back to being okay with it. After the initial shock and anger of finding out about Matt, she'd actually started to grieve a little. Not that she was in love, but, for the first time in a long time, it felt possible.

And that didn't happen in Bonne Terre very often. Not for her.

But she was over it. A week after Matt had been revealed as a fraud, she was her old self again.

"I still don't understand why you let him stay. I thought you were going to run him out of town for sure."

"Not my call, sadly," Savannah said.

Juliette snorted, speaking volumes in the language between friends.

"What is your point?" Savannah asked.

"If you really wanted him gone, he'd be gone."

"Margot may be old, but she's no pushover, and she wanted him to stay." Juliette was silent, and again, the silence said plenty. "I'm serious."

"Fine. Play that way." Juliette shrugged and tossed a handful of candy into her mouth. She twisted on the printer table to better watch whatever Matt was doing. "He doesn't look healthy."

Savannah thought the same thing, but she stayed mute. No way was she admitting she'd been watching him.

Not at first, of course—she'd stayed strong for two days. But then she'd noticed that the sounds of work coming from the courtyard didn't stop. Ever. They started at dawn and ended at dusk without break.

It had turned into some kind of contest. If he was working, she was working. The sounds of saws and hammers became an odd soundtrack to religious rituals around the world, and watching him from the corner of her eye became her new hobby.

Thanks to his insane work schedule, the Discovery work was done three days before she had to go back to the library. And she had a headache from glancing at him sideways.

"Jeez," Juliette whispered through her teeth. "He looks like he's lost about five pounds."

"He doesn't eat," Savannah said. "Margot leaves out sandwiches for lunch, but he eats them for dinner and I don't know what he's doing in the morning."

Juliette smirked at her. "I knew you cared."

"I don't," Savannah insisted. "But the Notorious O'Neills don't need him dying on our property."

"Good point," Juliette said, looking out the window again. "At least he's drinking water."

"Oh, he's plenty hydrated. Around noon, Katie sits up in the cypress and throws water balloons at him. It used to be orange peels, but yesterday she upped her game."

"You don't feel like stopping that?"

"I feel like filling up the balloons for her."

Juliette watched him out the window for a long moment. "He is one good-looking guy. You sure you don't want to give me a few details of whatever you two did in the library—"

"Did you have a point in coming here?" Savannah knew Juliette was trying to get her to snap, but she refused to take the bait.

"A friend can't stop by and lust after the help?"

Savannah rolled her eyes. "Just a second," she murmured and attached the last file. Satisfaction brewed in her as she clicked the Send button and rolled away from her desk, grabbing a bag of candy as she went.

Nothing said celebration like stale candy.

"I did come for a reason," Juliette said, swinging around to face Savannah. Juliette was in police-chief mode and it made Savannah's heart sink.

"I talked to Garrett's and Owen's folks. The boys insist they didn't have anything to do with either break-in."

"Of course they didn't." Savannah scowled, splitting a red chocolate between her teeth.

"The parents weren't much help, but a certain vibe I got from Garrett's stepmom makes me believe they weren't so innocent regarding the first incident with the spray paint."

"There's nothing you can do?" Savannah knew the answer even as she asked it.

"Not without proof, sorry. But we'll keep an eye on them."

Savannah smiled, grim and weary. "You did the best you could."

"The good news is, the whole town knows about Matt living here, so I'd imagine the break-ins will stop."

"That's my silver lining?"

"Well, that and being able to watch him out your window. Seriously, he's sexy as hell."

Savannah took a deep breath and gave in to her raging curiosity. "So? What did you find out about him?" There was only one question she really needed answered.

Juliette looked blank. "What do you mean?"

"Matt Woods—you wrote down all that information."

Juliette laughed. "I didn't do anything with it. The guy was clearly telling the truth. I've never seen a more tortured liar in my life. You could tell it doesn't come easily to him."

"He didn't seem to have any problem the night before," Savannah murmured. But then, she wondered, maybe all that stuff he'd said in the library was the truth. The mother dying of cancer and his friend, Jack.

Not that she cared.

"You're the researcher," Juliette said. "I thought for sure you'd have him all vetted by now." Juliette stared at her wide-eyed. "You haven't searched his name on the Internet? You? You don't buy dishwasher detergent without looking it up on the Internet."

"I've been busy."

"Sure you have."

Again, that silence that seemed to say so much.

"You know," Juliette said, softly, carefully, as if she knew she was tiptoeing onto thin ice, "the chance of him being married—"

"I know," Savannah said, but she couldn't calm the voices screaming *what if?*

"Is that why you haven't checked him out?"

"I don't think I could survive that again," Savannah said, locked up in knots. Ridiculous, as if that particular lightning would strike twice, but she was still scared of typing Matt's name into a search engine and seeing that picture of the perfect family with Matt's name in the caption.

The memory of doing just that eight years ago still had the power to bottom out her stomach. "My conscience is about maxed out."

"You can't still be blaming yourself about Eric. He didn't tell you," Juliette cried.

"It's my job, Juliette, to find things out. It's what I do."

"But why would you even suspect—"

"Doesn't change anything," Savannah said, guilt like a nice warm blanket she curled up with now and again.

"It changes everything. You like being a martyr." Juliette stood, repositioning her gun and badge on her hip. "When you finally get around to finding out who's living in your house, find out why he got so gung ho about those gems six months ago."

"He told us," Savannah said. "His father had just confessed the truth about the theft."

Juliette shook her head. "I checked Joel Woods out. That man did six and a half years of quiet time. He's out in six months and *now* he talks? And not to the cops or his lawyer, but to his architect son. Why?"

"What's your police brain thinking?"

"Either, something happened recently that got Matt all fired up and sent him down here like a late vigilante—"

"Or?"

Juliette grabbed another bag of candy. "Or he wants the jewels for himself."

THE SUN HAD SET a long time ago and shadows chased Savannah through the kitchen that smelled like the gumbo they'd had for dinner.

There was a plastic container of leftovers in the fridge and she could grab it and take it out to him as easily as not. But she chose not.

He didn't deserve gumbo.

She found him in the dark twilight, working on the last of the greenhouse, carefully sliding glass panes into place. His back rippled, the small muscles of his arms flexed and shifted as he built a house of glass.

He had lost weight—the side of his face that she could see was thin. His cheekbones looked like they could cut steaks.

Not that she cared, but seriously, they didn't need him passing out or worse.

"You should eat," she said and he jumped, nearly dropping a pane on his feet.

"Christ," he breathed. "You shouldn't sneak up on people."

She crossed her arms over her chest, and tried very hard to convince herself that she didn't want to touch him. Didn't want to stroke back the sweaty hunk of hair that fell over his forehead, practically into his eyes.

He needed a haircut.

Not. That. I. Care.

"I have a question," she said.

He grunted, picking up another glass square, unwrapping it from its protective shell. His hands were raw, and a scrape along his palm was bleeding, probably going to get infected.

Not. That. I. Care.

"Are you here because you want the jewels for your-self?"

That got his attention and he straightened to his full height. He was a big man, over six feet. Strong, his T-shirt clinging to hard, lean muscles. Her nerve endings remembered what her flesh had felt like against those muscles, how all that contact had sent an electrical charge through the dormant parts of her body. Waking her up. Turning her on.

"No," he said, wiping his hands on his shirt, leaving smears of dirt and blood. "I don't care about the gems."

"Where are your gloves?" she snapped, angry that he was dumb enough to do this work without protection and angry that she cared.

"They have a hole."

"Get a new pair."

His lips twisted slightly. "Yes, boss."

He slid the glass home.

"So if you're not here for the diamond and ruby, why come seven years after the fact?"

He bent and picked up a broken pane and cursed under his breath before carefully setting the pieces into what she assumed was the junk pile. Concrete, glass, bits of brick and stacks of ruin, like terrible, shattered buildings.

His silence stretched and pulled until Savannah snapped. "You lied your way into our home. We have a right to know."

He breathed something she didn't hear as he bent to pick up another pane.

"What?"

"Justice!" he yelled, glass shattering at their feet. She jumped at the sound and the sudden fury in his voice.

"Dad didn't do the crime alone, his hands weren't the only ones dirty."

"But it's seven years too late—"

"Guilt should be punished."

The courtyard rang with his voice and she stepped back, stunned. Something else was at work here, she could see it in his face. Feel it in the air around him, smell it like sulfur and blood.

"I'm sorry," he said, his voice suspiciously calm. But she could see, in the moonlight, his heartbeat throbbing in his neck, as if he'd been running for miles.

"Are you okay?" she asked, and hated herself for asking.

"Sure," he answered, but he was lying. An idiot could see he was lying.

She had questions. Plenty of them. A thin river of concern running through them all but, finally, she decided to listen to herself.

She didn't care.

She walked to the house but stopped at the door. She tore chunks of chipped white paint from the door frame, flicking them away with her thumb.

"Are you married?" she asked.

A sound like laughter or a growl rumbled up his throat and she felt it in her spine, her belly.

"Just answer the question."

"No," he said, his voice thick and solid.

"I can find out if you're lying."

"Then why ask?"

She didn't say anything, the memories and shame and guilt making her nauseous. She rested her head against the screen door, hating that the worst thing she'd ever done had brought her Katie, the best thing that had ever happened to her.

"I'm not married," he said, softly.

"Good." She pushed the word past the ball of sick in her

throat. She stepped through the door and stopped again, sympathy and a dozen other things she didn't want to examine too closely stopping her feet.

"There's gumbo in the fridge," she said. She listened to the humming silence behind her for a moment and went inside.

IT WAS EASY, in the end.

She sat in her dark ridiculous bed, moonlight splashed across her lap and the computer cradled there, her finger poised over the enter key.

Matt Woods typed into the search engine.

No matter what he said, Matt was absolutely not okay. She didn't want to see it, but it was like watching someone self-destruct right in front of your eyes. Something was eating him, from the inside out.

Guilt deserves to be punished.

She had the terrible suspicion that Matt was using her courtyard as punishment.

But for what?

Without a second thought, Savannah hit the enter key.

"Matt Woods receives award," she muttered, reading the files. "Woods Takes On Downtown. Architect Has 'Elemental' Vision For The City. Contractor begins work on billion-dollar rejuvenation."

And finally:

"Tragedy!"

She followed that link, her heart in her throat, to a three-page article in the *Post-Dispatch*.

The grand opening of Matt Woods's new Elements Building ended in tragedy last night when twenty-eight-year-old Peter Borjat died in the partial building collapse.

Savannah sat back, feeling as if she'd swallowed rocks.

Instead of a picture of a happy family including Matt, what she saw was somehow worse. A haunting picture of a wide-open room with gabled ceilings and skylights, soaring steel girders and polished pine floors. Chandeliers glittered and cocktail tables still held half-filled martini glasses, as though the drinkers had just gone to the bathroom. A woman's red high heel lay next to a gaping, jagged hole in the corner. A curvy steel sculpture jutted out of the black crater like a horrific swizzle stick.

She clicked onto the second page.

Officials now say that the floor collapse was caused by poor construction. The remodel of the two-hundred-year-old warehouse was incomplete and insufficient for the planned usage of the space. According to investigators, the floor in question was not properly reinforced.

"The lives of everyone at that party were in jeopardy," Inspector Phillip Jefferson states. "It's a blessing there weren't more deaths."

"The plans for that particular space were changed last minute," Jack Donnelly said in a written statement. "That, however is no excuse for what I did and I take full responsibility."

A picture was coming together in Savannah's mind and it wasn't pretty. Poor construction? The death of a twenty-eight-year-old man?

Her stomach twisted and churned, acid rising in her throat.

And she thought *her* demons were bad?

Matt had blood on his hands.

However, the next story muddied the picture in her mind.

Architect Proves No Knowledge of Poor Construction.

In deposition today, Matt Woods proved he had no knowledge of what his partner and longtime friend Jack Donnelly was doing to cut costs in the construction of the Elements Building.

Woods, who has been unreachable since the tragedy, appeared grief-stricken and shocked outside the courtroom. Despite the ruling, he defended Donnelly.

"What happened," Woods said, "was my fault as much as it was Jack's. This was a partnership. My condolences and sincere regret go out to Peter's family and friends. I know there is nothing I can do to repair your loss and I am deeply sorry for my role in this tragedy."

Savannah rubbed her hands over her face.
Hero? she wondered. *Or bad guy?*
There was only one way to find out.

CHAPTER ELEVEN

MATT DIDN'T KNOW WHAT time it was. The sky was bruised, but pink touched the eastern clouds so he figured it was close enough to day to get to work.

He rose from the chair he'd spent the night in and pulled on the clean clothes that Margot laundered for him at the end of each day. He barely felt the denim and cotton. Or the sting of his blistered palms. He was dimly aware of an ache in his stomach, but food, he'd learned, wasn't going down so well these days.

He filled his thermos with water in the bathroom and stepped outside into the hot liquid kiss of a Louisiana summer morning.

All of it, the burn of his tired and sore muscles, the heat of the day, the buzz of insects, seemed somehow removed, disconnected from him.

Instead, his ears roared with the screams of metal and the thundering splinter of wood.

"Matt?"

Everything went silent at the sound of Savannah's voice. He turned looking for her in the shadows, wondering if this was another figment of his imagination.

Another ghost coming to get a piece of him.

He glanced down and realized he was standing right next to her. Savannah sat on the steps, her bare legs, honey-colored and long as the horizon, curled up to her chest.

Her eyes, wide and liquid in the dark, looked up at him. Right through him.

She knows. The thought was like a gong in his empty chest. It made sense, of course—she was a researcher and his crimes were hardly hidden.

"I brought coffee," she said, holding out a mug.

It smelled good, bitter and dark. His body practically screamed for the caffeine.

"No thanks," he said, stepping past her toward the courtyard. She brought the coffee because she wanted to talk. And he wanted to start digging trenches for the box hedge maze.

"Matt," she said, that Southern accent winding through the courtyard to curl around in and around him, like smoke from some internal fire. "I know about the accident."

He didn't answer, just opened the shed and started taking out his tools. Dawn was approaching and the dark night was turning gray.

"Did you know?" she asked from a few feet away. "About the floors?"

Did I know? Strange that everyone thought that knowledge meant guilt. Or that lack of knowledge meant innocence. As if it were that easy.

"Does it matter?" he asked, kicking a clod of dirt off the sharp edge of his shovel then throwing it on the ground.

"Of course—"

"I don't want to talk about this, Savannah." He gave her a hard look.

"Well, if you want to keep punishing yourself in my courtyard, you're going to have to talk."

He ducked farther into the shed, grabbing the hand tools.

"I'm not going to leave this alone," she said, from the doorway.

Of course not. Of course she'd make this hard.

"It's none of your business." He growled the words, stomping past her to the cypress.

"You're right," she said. "It's not. But Jack—"

"How about we talk about Katie's father?" he asked, shifting to offense, his temper lit. "Where is he?" She went pale and he arched his eyebrows, waiting. Feeling relentless, he wanted to hammer on her like the ghosts hammered on him.

A mourning dove cooed and a dog barked someplace close by and he waited. He waited and he watched her, remembering the way she tasted. Wanting suddenly, ferociously, to taste her again. To lose himself in all the promised heat that still lingered between them.

Hotter now, this moment, her lips a trembling bow, than ever.

"Go to hell, Matt," she snapped. She spun on her heel and left.

I already am, he thought, and started digging holes.

NINE HOURS LATER, Matt put the tools away, his work for the day done. The heat had been relentless today. So thick, so heavy it dragged at his limbs, sucked at his head. Katie's midafternoon water balloon shower had been a fantastic relief. He'd thanked her, which got him the scowling of a lifetime.

He shut the door to the shed and his vision swam, the earth dipped under his feet. Luckily, the shed was there to hold him up.

"You're eating with us tonight."

He forced the world to right itself and his vision to clear. When he was sure he wouldn't fall over, he turned.

Margot looked regal in pressed linen, a red scarf around her hair. Diamonds sparkled at her ears.

"Is that an order, Margot?"

"Damn right it is. I didn't ask you to stay so you could kill yourself."

"For a group of women so angry with me, you're awfully concerned about my welfare."

"And I'm tired of living with martyrs. We're eating in an hour." Margot's eyes raked over him. "Clean yourself up."

SAVANNAH COULD NOT LEAVE IT ALONE. Matt and the Elements Building tragedy were like a sore tooth she couldn't keep her tongue away from.

Hours passed in a few clicks of her mouse.

With each story she read, her pendulum regarding Matt swung back and forth between hero and bad guy, lingering more and more on hero.

He didn't know about the floors. Research rarely lied and the research proved it.

During the final push of the construction, he'd been in Moscow, then Nebraska. Peter Borjat, who'd died in the accident, was also the sculptor whose work was being shown in that fatal corner. He was supposed to be showing a piece made of glass and pine at the opening, but it had sold two weeks before the party.

Instead, they subbed an iron-and-steel piece of his that weighed a ton. The contractor, Jack, wasn't informed until two nights before the event.

It was a small detail compared to the thousand bigger ones the men were handling leading up to the gala. It had been dealt with by assistants and subcontractors, and by the time word got to Jack and Matt, it was too late.

Jack, as he said in his deposition, had crossed his fingers and prayed. Clearly, it hadn't worked.

Peter's family hadn't pressed charges against Jack and

152 THE TEMPTATION OF SAVANNAH O'NEILL

Matt, but the cleanup and recovery costs had bankrupted Jack, who, even before taking on the Elements Building, had been having a tough year.

In the six months since the tragedy, Matt had opened a fund for Peter Borjat's family. Given a few more hours, she'd probably be able to find out how much he'd donated.

Savannah closed her computer. She didn't want to feel this way about Matt. Sympathy, empathy, whatever this was, she didn't want it.

It made her chest hurt.

Asking her about Katie's father had been a low blow, but considering the depth and breadth of his guilt—similar in size, she imagined, to her own—she would have done the same thing.

"Mom!" Katie cried from the bottom of the stairs. "Dinner!"

Ugh, Savannah thought, twisting her hair up on her head in a sloppy bun. It was almost too hot to eat.

Rising reluctantly, she pulled on a clean tank top and changed from cutoffs to a light pink skirt. It wasn't quite dressing for dinner, but at least Margot wouldn't lecture her.

She met Katie at the bottom of the stairs.

"He's here," Katie said, with a scowl fit for any bad guy in the movies, which was a pretty good indicator of who *he* was. "Margot invited him."

"Then we will be polite," Savannah said, rubbing a hand over Katie's head. Her little girl continued to scowl. "I don't know why you're so mad at him."

"Because you are," Katie said. "Or you were."

"Let's try to keep an open mind," she said, tucking her arm around Katie and heading toward the dining room. Something that felt like excitement tingled along her skin.

She told herself it wasn't the prospect of being close to Matt again. It was this mystery that was so thrilling, her O'Neill curiosity curse was all atingle because his grief was fascinating.

He was just a handsome man.

And he was truly handsome. As Savannah stepped into the dining room, he looked up from where he sat at Margot's left and her heart hammered inside her chest.

His face was deeply tanned from working outside, except for small wrinkles and creases around his eyes that somehow made him more attractive. His hair had lightened from mahogany to oak and against all that tan skin his eyes were the brilliant color of spring grass.

"Hello, Savannah," he said, his voice like a rough tongue licking her stomach.

"Matt," she said brusquely, which wasn't what she wanted. So she smiled, briefly, awkwardly, to smooth her rough edges.

Katie stuck out her tongue.

"Don't," Savannah said in her stern mommy voice, and Katie flounced to her seat at Margot's right.

The atmosphere in the room was strange and volatile. Cold winds, warm breezes and a great dark cloud where Matt sat.

Savannah had no clue how to make any of it better.

"Now," Margot said, her smile wide and gracious. "Isn't this nice."

IT WAS HELL.

Matt could not take his eyes off Savannah. This version of her, slightly messy, almost undone—God, it was such a surprise. Such a turn-on.

He felt like a fourteen-year-old boy. And, even in his exhausted state, his body was reacting like a fourteen-year-old's and he wanted to dump the cold Thai noodle salad right into his lap.

"Are you enjoying the dinner, Matt?" Margot asked.

"It's delicious," he said, and it was, he'd just prefer to eat Savannah. But he lifted a cold shrimp and a bunch of herby green things to his mouth.

"It's one of Savannah's specialties," Margot said, inclining her head toward Savannah where she sat at the foot of the table. Seriously, Margot was, like, old-world charming. They simply didn't make them like her anymore.

"No, it's not," Savannah said, laughing slightly. She turned to Matt, her blue eyes hesitantly warm, cautious but friendly. In a glance, he realized that's exactly how she was—a warm fire, banked.

Suddenly he wished she'd answered that question about Katie's father, because every instinct told him he was the man who'd banked her fire.

Which was a crime, really.

"I don't cook," Savannah said. "She's trying to matchmake."

He choked on the shrimp.

"Don't worry," Savannah said, shooting her grandmother a knock-it-off look. "It's compulsive. Like lying. She can't help herself."

"It's a gift," Margot said.

"A curse," Savannah interjected.

"Tell that to John F. Kennedy."

"John F. *who?*" Matt asked.

"Kennedy," Margot said.

"Margot," Savannah said, taking the reins of the story, "claims to have introduced JFK to Marilyn Monroe."

"You've got to be kidding me," he said, laughing despite himself.

"Hardly," Margot answered. "I knew Marilyn through Arthur—"

"Miller?" he asked, astounded.

"He was a good friend for a number of years," Margot answered with a glint in her eye.

"She's always been a patron of the arts," Savannah said with a wicked smile.

"No need to be crude," Margot chastised. "He was a dear friend and Marilyn was a lovely, if slightly tortured girl."

"But how did you know the president?" Matt asked.

"He was a friend, too. Although that was before he was president."

His fork clattered to his plate. He'd known she'd run in high and varied circles, but *JFK?* He glanced at Savannah, wondering if he wasn't being put on. Just a little.

As if she read his mind, she nodded her head. "All true, I'm afraid. She put the Notorious in the O'Neills."

"Not all by myself," Margot said, her look pointed, and Savannah wiped her mouth discreetly and focused on eating.

The tension in the room returned, prickly and aware.

Forks hitting plates and Katie quietly slurping noodles were the only noises. Savannah's warmth was all but gone; a chill blew off her. Blew off all of them. He realized he should leave, so the women could go back to doing what they normally did when he wasn't here to ruin dinner.

But the sleeping porch had no appeal right now. None. Hot, dark and lonely. And sitting here was—well, it was fun.

He had no reason to stay other than he enjoyed it. And

it had been a long long time since his only motivation was enjoyment.

"I designed a house for a certain famous couple," he said, the words falling out of him and popping the tension. Three pairs of feminine and fascinated eyes swung to him. Even Katie put her hostility away as they cajoled the names of the pair from him.

"Really?" Savannah asked.

"Do tell," Margot insisted. "Is he as handsome in real life?"

"More so," Matt answered. "They're both beautiful. Ridiculously beautiful. I would marry him." His honesty earned him a round of jokes about him in a white dress.

He had seconds, then thirds of the salad as he answered their questions about designing for the fabulously wealthy. Savannah brought out dishes of lime sherbet and Matt got Margot to tell him about her brief affair with a certain Bond actor.

"Let's just say," Margot said, eyebrow cocked as she stood to clear the dishes, "he took the James Bond thing very seriously. If you know what I mean."

"Margot," Savannah groaned, picking up a stack of bowls and taking them into the kitchen.

"What does she mean?" Katie asked, her eyes dancing between the adults.

"Here," Matt said, standing up to grab the rest of the dishes before Margot got to them. "Let me help."

Margot grabbed his hand and turned it over. The blisters and scrapes on his palm looked red and angry in the bright light of the chandelier. "You're doing enough," Margot said softly. "I don't know what demon has possessed—"

He pulled his hands free and grabbed the plates anyway. "I'm fine," he said. "Let me make my mother proud and clear the table."

Margot lifted her hands in surrender and sat.

"Well, then," she said, "perhaps we can go back to our game? Katie and I have grown bored playing with just the two of us."

"Sure," he said, happy at the thought.

"No." Katie stood. "I won't play with him." She ran from the room.

"Katie!" Margot called after her.

"No," he said, something dark and heavy sitting on his chest. Regret? Grief? Probably both. "Don't worry about it. I've still got a lot of work to do. It's probably best."

Matt grabbed the empty salad bowl and took it into the kitchen. There was no dishwasher, and Savannah was filling the sink with bubbles.

"I'll wash, you dry?" she asked.

He met her gaze; so blue and careful. Cautious, as if she expected rejection.

Suddenly the kitchen was too small and he wanted badly to escape to the courtyard. To be alone. The temptation of her was nearly too much, but in the end he merely nodded and stepped aside so she could stand at the sink.

Because he was a glutton for punishment, and because a few hours in the company of these women made him feel lighter. Cleaner. The ghosts and their dirty hands were leaving him alone.

They worked silently, each of them careful not to touch one another in handing off dishes. Not that it particularly mattered. Touching or not, he wanted her so bad he could taste it. Like lime sherbet on his tongue.

"Tell me something," she said, handing him a dinner plate. "Did you lie about your mother?"

He knew exactly what she meant—that night in the library when she'd laid herself so bare.

I should lie now, he thought. Tell her that everything he said that night had been a lie, that it had all been designed to get her to talk to him.

He opened his mouth to do it, to drive her away for good.

But he glanced down at her exposed neck. The pale skin stretched over fine muscles. The wisps of blond hair there, too short to be pulled into a ponytail. He wanted to touch that hair, see if it was as soft as it looked. He wanted to press his lips to the dip at the top of her spine. He wanted to curl his arms around her taut body, cup her breasts in his hands, press himself along her back.

He wanted to wrap himself around her and never let go.

"Nothing I said that night was a lie," he answered. "My mom, Dad—" he stumbled slightly "—Jack. All of it was the truth."

She blinked at him, her eyes warm, her lips so full and pink he wanted to chew on them.

"Thank you," she whispered.

He leaned toward her, ready to take her up on the invitation in her trembling lips and liquid eyes. He remembered how she'd felt in his arms, how she had the power to banish his ghosts, and he suddenly wanted that again. Craved it with every aching and sore muscle in his body.

Solace, she offered solace.

"Matt!" Margot called from the other room and Savannah jerked away, scrubbing with renewed vigor.

"Don't keep the queen waiting," Savannah said, overly bright.

Unsure of what to say or do, he finally set down the towel and left the kitchen, his body getting cooler the farther he was from temptation.

SAVANNAH BRACED HER HANDS on the bottom of the sink, hot suds up to her elbows, and hung her head. Matt was potent medicine and he went right to her head, erasing every sane thought she had.

Researching him had to stop. As did the temptation to make out with him in the kitchen.

Even if he had told her the truth, even if he was so wounded she could see the scars in his eyes, even if he was charming and handsome and fun, he would still hurt her.

Because at some point, Matt would leave.

Eventually, everyone left her.

She finished the dishes and even managed to persuade Katie to help put away the dry ones before she rushed off to finish her puzzle with Margot.

Savannah poured herself a cold glass of water and was about to go upstairs when the music started.

Matt was playing the piano. "Ode to Joy," which seemed sad and ironic considering the grief he carried. The music filled the hallways, brushed the ceilings, twisted and turned and curved around her heart until she was in knots.

She sat on the steps, powerless against Matt and his sad music.

CHAPTER TWELVE

Matt woke up, blinking into hot sunshine, stunned to realize he'd actually slept.

And from the angle of the sun shining directly into his eyes, he'd say he overslept. He pulled on clean clothes and filled his thermos. At the last minute, he grabbed a notebook and pencil so he could sketch out the final pattern for the maze.

He'd been thinking in terms of right angles. Squares in squares. But last night he'd dreamt in circles.

Harder to pull off, but infinitely more interesting.

Once outside, he saw his kingdom had been overrun. The shed doors were open, the tools haphazardly laid out and Savannah, in cutoffs and a black tank top that hugged every curve and muscle in her body like a shadow, was in jeopardy of cutting off her own hand with the bush trimmers.

"What are you doing?" he asked.

She whirled, slicing the air with razor-sharp blades. "Hey, Matt. Since someone decided to sleep in, I thought I'd do a little work—"

He yanked the trimmers from her hands and put them on the ground, arranging things so they lay between the hoe and the ax.

It was stupid, this irrational proprietary urge he had. It wasn't even his courtyard. It was hers. She could pave the damn thing if she wanted.

"I only trimmed the cypress," she said, annoyed. "I've managed the middle courtyard for twenty years, it's not like I'm going to ruin anything."

You're ruining everything, he thought.

"I'm used to working alone," he said, trying to sound as unfriendly as possible.

"I understand," she said, putting her hands on her impossibly thin waist. She really was like a willow. So beautiful, but strong. "That's how I work, too." She grabbed a thermos of coffee that had been resting in the grass and held it out to him. "Here. Peace."

Part of him resisted, knowing that if he wanted her to keep her distance, this wasn't exactly the way to go about it.

"It's just coffee," she said, again as if she could read his mind, and it was so oddly intimate, he couldn't resist.

A great ache yawned inside of him, a loneliness.

I miss Jack, he realized. He missed having friends and people in his life. His father, the prince of thieves, sitting in the visiting room at Martinsville Prison so eager for company. Erica, bringing him coffee and office gossip while doing the job of twenty people. And Jack—

"You all right?" Savannah asked.

He blinked, coming back to earth. "Fine." He took the coffee. "Thank you."

"So," Savannah said, looking around at the cleared-out courtyard. "What's the plan, Mr. Architect of the Year?"

"How did you find that out?" He laughed. Wow, winning that award seemed like a million years ago. Almost as though it had happened to a different guy. It had been so important, coming as it had right before the opening. Publicity, he'd thought, for the project of a lifetime.

"It's on your Web site," she said, shaking her head.

"Boy, you've really dropped right out of your life, haven't you?"

He took a deep drink of the hot black coffee and didn't answer. The answer was all too obvious.

I wonder how many voice mails I have from Erica, now?

He was stunned to realize he wanted to check. He wanted to look at his old life for the first time in months.

Something was happening here, at this house. He was growing back into his old skin.

"I finished my research work two days ago and I'm not scheduled to be back in the library until tomorrow, so I thought I'd lend a hand. And—" she smiled "—I'm guessing you probably don't want or need my help and are trying to figure out how to get rid of me. But sadly, my daughter gets her stubbornness from me."

And I'm not going anywhere. The words rang in his head as if she'd yelled them rather than implied them.

He wondered if she was here with the foolish idea that she could save him, and he wanted to tell her not to bother.

"I'm building a maze," he said. He set down the thermos and pulled the pencil and notebook out of his back pocket. "I was thinking something…" He began sketching. Beginning with the cypress in the center, he worked his way out, creating blind alleys and hidey-holes that went nowhere. All in a circular pattern. "I was thinking box hedges, but that won't really work with the form. I'll need to—"

"Lilacs," she said. "Here." She pointed to his sketch, the dark outer perimeter of his circles. "And honeysuckle, for the inside."

It clicked. "That would be—"

"Smelly?" she asked, with a laugh.

"Perfect," he said, getting lost for a moment in her eyes. "Totally perfect."

He didn't know how long they stood that way. A second, ten minutes. But time collapsed, disappeared, and all there was were her eyes, blue as the sky and bottomless.

"Matt," she breathed. "Tell me about the accident."

He went cold. Numb. In a heartbeat.

He stepped away, throwing the sketch on the ground and reaching for the tools. She got in his way, her hands, so delicate and clean on his, and he recoiled from the contact.

"You didn't know about the floors," she whispered.

He took tiny sips of air because there was suddenly a shortage.

"Did you?"

"It doesn't matter," he said. "Not to Pete Borjat. Not to his girlfriend."

"But there was nothing you could have done, Matt."

"I could have opened my eyes and seen the problems Jack was having instead of stupidly, blindly following my own vision."

He stepped into the shed, grabbing equipment, needing to do something, anything, because the pressure in his head and body was about to burst.

"Did he tell you he didn't reinforce the floors there?"

"No, but the building was in much worse shape than anyone thought. I knew he'd downgraded some of the supplies." Matt threw more and more tools onto the ground, pitching them in anger, hurling things he didn't need to feed his impulse for violence. "He told me over and over again that he could not take another loss. That he could not afford my visions. My obsessions."

"But if he didn't tell you, it's not your fault—" Suddenly she stopped, blinked, her mouth gaping.

He pulled out more tools and her silence continued. She stood there, a deer in headlights, her face white with shock.

"Savannah," he asked. "You all right?"

She shook her head and he stepped to her side, slid his hand over her shoulder for support.

She put her hands over her face and remained still for a long time, so long Matt got worried and looked over her shoulder for any sign of Margot.

"My grandmother has been telling me the same thing for years," she said. "It's not my fault because I didn't know. Years of her saying that and then you come here, with your guilt and your lies, and it all makes sense."

She lifted her pale face to his, her eyes burning and wet with unshed tears, her lips a white line.

"What's not your fault?" he asked.

"You asked me about Katie's father." Her voice was a whisper, thick and ragged.

He nodded, speechless.

"Years ago, he hired me to do some research. He was working on a documentary about Creole music and culture. I did the work and as a side note told him he should come to Bonne Terre, to see Remy's. It's a club out in the bayou about ten miles south of here." She took a deep breath and it shuddered at the top. "He came. Fell in love with the place and decided to change the focus of the documentary to Remy, fourth-generation Remy, who still runs the place."

Matt squeezed her shoulder, seeing how this might pan out.

"We started...dating." Her smile was sharp, bitter. Loaded with all the things she didn't need to say about those dates. "And in time, I told him he should stay at the Manor. He stayed on and off for three months and I—" She shook her head and looked at her hands, unfurling them to reveal moon-shaped divots made by her nails. He wanted to kiss those divots. Kiss every pain she ever felt. "I was stupid in love. Stupid. And I thought he was, too. So, when I got pregnant, I thought it would all work out."

"It didn't."

"He was married. He had two children in Chicago."

He closed his eyes and swore.

She laughed, a brittle, slightly hysterical sound. "I've blamed myself for nine years. Every whisper behind my back. Every slur painted on our walls, I've accepted them as payment for my sins."

"But you didn't know," Matt said.

"I'm a researcher, Matt. Finding out is what I do. I let myself get taken. Not like you."

She reached up and touched his fingers, lacing hers between his, strong and fragile at the same time. Their palms touched, her heartbeat pulsed against his skin. The urge to pull her close, bend that strong body against his was like a riptide, pulling him places he had no business going.

"If he didn't tell you, you couldn't know, Matt. It wasn't your job. You can stop blaming yourself for something you had no control over."

"It's not the same thing," he said, shaking his hands free.

"It's not?"

"Lives are ruined!" he yelled. "Peter is dead. His girlfriend is alone. Jack is bankrupt."

"Not your fault," she said. "It's a tragedy, no doubt about it, but you didn't cause it. This guilt you're carrying—" she shook her head "—it's not yours."

"Someone should be punished."

"The world doesn't work that way, Matt."

"Well, the world doesn't always get it right." Matt ducked into the shed, pulling out two pairs of gloves. He tugged on the ones with the hole and gave her the new pair. "You can work," he said, "but I'm done talking."

SAVANNAH HEARD Katie up in the tree, getting ready with her water balloon arsenal. Funny, Savannah thought, wiping the sweaty hair off her forehead, three days ago she wanted to hurl the water balloons herself.

She glanced over at Matt where he knelt on the ground, measuring trenches like graves.

Now, she didn't know what she wanted. But it was time to stop Katie's attacks on the poor guy. Lord knows he suffered enough at his own hands without Katie's help.

"Katie!" she cried, just in time to halt the yellow balloon lifted in her little hand. "I need to talk to you inside."

"But, Mom—"

She put down the shovel and stepped over to the tree, peering up into the branches at her daughter's red round face.

"Inside," she said. "Now."

Matt's attention, his gaze, his presence ten feet behind her was as tangible as a hand at her back. She didn't turn around, wasn't ready to meet those green eyes. She was still too raw and vulnerable, her world still unsure without the guilt she'd carried for so long.

She felt slightly newer, somehow. Her skin fragile in the sunlight without the heavy protection of her hair shirt.

Katie scrambled down from the tree, grumbling the whole time, and Savannah followed her into the house.

"This stuff with Matt has to stop," she said, once they got into the kitchen.

"What stuff?" Katie asked, blinking her eyes at Savannah.

"Don't be cute," Savannah snapped. "I've let you run wild around here for too long. Now, I want you to stop with the water balloons and the attitude."

"We thought he was our friend and he lied to us, Mom!"

Oh, how to explain to her daughter the many shades of gray. "I know." She sighed. "But—"

"He made you cry!" Katie yelled. "And now you're out there like he's a friend."

"Maybe he is—"

"No!"

Savannah realized there was something else at work here, something more than retaliating at Matt for lying to them.

"We don't need friends, Mom! We just need each other, right? That's what you've always said. All we need is each other."

Savannah blinked, stunned. "Katie, honey, it's not always going to be just us."

"Why not?" Katie asked. "It's been you, me and Margot for a long time and we're doing fine. Why do you want him here, anyway?"

Savannah had no answer. She couldn't even totally explain it to herself. But she liked him here. The past few hours, working silently side by side with him, had been the warmest in her memory.

She wanted to kiss him. She wanted to pull that strong body against hers and feel small. Feel cared for. Womanly and precious.

She wanted Matt, with his lies and guilt, she wanted him still. More, maybe, now that she knew the truth.

"You *like* him," Katie cried as though it was the crime of the century, the murder of innocents.

"I do," Savannah said, "but that doesn't mean I don't like you. Or—"

"Well, I don't like *you!*" She ran off down the dark hallway, her feet thundering up the stairs.

"She's just like you" a deep male voice behind her said. A deep male voice Savannah hadn't heard in far too long.

"Carter!" she cried, whirling to face her big brother. One look at his handsome face, so strong and fierce, like a profile you'd see on an ancient coin, and she was ten years old again.

Tears suddenly burned at her eyes. The fact that he'd been gone so long, out of their lives, felt like a cut deep through her.

"It's been so long," she breathed, hearing the accusation in her voice.

Carter blinked, the charming smile slid off his face. "I've asked you to come visit," he said. "It's your choice—"

"This is your home," she said.

You are supposed to be here, she thought. *You are supposed to stay. We were all supposed to stay.*

But no one ever stayed. Ever.

Carter's smile was sad, but his arms opened and she stepped right into them. "I missed you, Savvy."

MATT COULD FEEL Katie up in that tree, despite the fact that there were no water balloons falling on his head. He could feel her like a storm coming down from Canada—cold winds and icy rain.

"I know you're mad at me," he said, sticking his shovel in the ground and propping his hands on its end.

"You don't know anything!" Katie screamed, water balloons pelting the ground and exploding at his feet.

"Your mom—"

Katie swung down from the tree like some wild red-headed monkey. "You don't know anything about my mom!" At her rage Matt stepped back.

"Okay, okay, hold on."

"You made her cry!" She swatted at his arms and legs and he attempted to step back but he landed in the trench and fell back, hauling Katie in with him. They both scrambled in the dirt and some of the steam leaked out of Katie.

He rolled onto his back, looked up at white clouds stretched thin across a blue sky.

"I didn't mean to," he said, turning his head to look at the girl. "I never meant to hurt her." He ducked his head to better see her face. "Or you."

She sniffed and brushed her nose with her forearm.

"Tell you what," he said. "Tonight I'll show you how I beat you at poker."

She sniffed again and looked at him, her eyes so like her mother's, damning. "No," she said. She stood, pinning him to the ground with a whole bunch of eight-year-old anger. "If you don't want to hurt us, then leave. Right now. It'll only be worse if you stay."

She left, running past the cypress into the shadows at the back of the courtyard.

Guilt and loss, terrible things he'd done to people because he was blind, obsessed, these things were built like a brick wall around him. The whole world on the other side. For six months he'd been building this wall, craving this solitude.

He stood and brushed off his pants, glancing toward the house in time to see through one of the windows Savannah hurl herself into a man's arms.

Something dark and gritty rolled through him.

But then the man turned and he recognized Carter O'Neill from the surveillance photos.

But the gritty bit—like dirt and stones rattling through his guts and blood—stayed, reminding him that he had pushed away and hurt everyone who would welcome him like that.

Especially Savannah, and he felt the loss like a punch in the stomach.

CHAPTER THIRTEEN

"I GOT YOUR E-MAIL," Carter said, keeping his arm tucked tight around Savannah as they walked through the halls. Savannah didn't let go of Carter. Wouldn't for the world. He was here. Her brother was back.

"Before you get upset," Savannah said, pulling him into the kitchen because she was starving. "Margot is not quite as sick as I might have made out in my e-mail."

"Really?" Carter asked, grinning as he leaned against the counter.

"She's healthy as a damn horse. And Katie is not threatening to run away to see you."

"Somehow I figured. Where is Margot?"

"Church."

"Church?" Carter asked, astonished. Understandable, since Margot had never been one for religion. She'd always said that she sizzled when the priests splashed the holy water.

"Her latest is apparently a believer."

"This is the guy who took her on that cruise?"

"The same. She spends every Sunday with him and about once a month she's gone for a few days. They travel."

"A multimillionaire believer with a mistress?"

"Companion," Savannah corrected, using Margot's steel-and-petal tone. "Mistress is so gauche."

Carter laughed. "Only in Bonne Terre."

"Please," Savannah scoffed. "Like you don't have worse in the big city."

"You heard from Tyler?" he asked, changing the subject.

She smiled, nodded. "He sent a huge bouquet of flowers when he won that poker thing."

"I got a box of cigars," Carter said.

"Well, that's good."

"Sure, you know Tyler. Money, women, good times. That's all that matters."

"If you talk to him like that, no wonder he doesn't come visit."

"Tyler doesn't come visit because he's too busy being the big man, Savannah." He scrubbed a hand over his face, and she was reminded of how much he used to worry about his siblings when they were still with their mother. The way he cared. "Tyler's not the boy we knew. Not anymore."

Savannah wanted to press for more details, but she let it go. She only had Carter for a little while, and she didn't want to spend that time fighting.

"Things seem to be going well for you," Savannah said, watching him out of the corner of her eye as she grabbed an apple from the fridge. "Mayor Pro Temp."

Carter nodded. "Thank you. I wish you'd come to visit. There's—"

"You hungry?" Savannah asked, pulling out some turkey and another apple and cheese, anything not to look at him.

"You planning on spending every minute of your life here?"

Maybe. "Of course not."

"Then come visit."

"When?" she asked, thunking the food down on the counter. "Katie's in school and Margot—"

"Is an adult. She just went to China or someplace. She doesn't expect you to grow old with her."

Savannah started to assemble sandwiches as if on a stopwatch.

"Savannah." He touched her hand, pulled the knife from her fingers and forced her to look at him. "She's not coming back. Mom—"

"I know that," Savannah snapped, pulling her hands free.

"Then why are you waiting around like she is?"

"I stopped waiting for Mom ten years ago. This is my life, Carter. My home. It's yours, too."

"No, Savannah, it's not. It never was. It's where I was left."

Savannah sucked in a terrible breath, her vision swimming with sudden anger. A lifetime of it.

"You think *you've* been left? Every single—" She stopped and went back to sandwich building.

"Savannah?"

"Forget it," she said and shook her head. She was not going to talk about this. Not going to enumerate every time that front door had shut behind someone she loved. Her mother, her brothers. Eric. And Matt, when he got around to going. Just thinking about it made her whole body hurt.

"The world is not going to hurt you, Savvy."

Savannah laughed, bitter sadness making her feel twice her age. "There's plenty going on here that could hurt me," she said and Matt's face was forefront in her mind. The sweat and the smiles, the way he made her feel, as though she'd been dipped in something sweet. That would all turn to pain when he left.

"What's this about break-ins?" Carter asked.

She told him the story, leaving out the part about Matt

on the summer porch. Her brother was sort of an old-world Southern gentleman, charming at a distance, but a hassle under the same roof.

"And the police think it's teenagers?" he asked, pulling his red silk tie free from his collar.

Savannah nodded.

"Is that what you think?" Carter asked.

"Yes…" She sighed. "Maybe. There's also this situation with some stolen gems. I don't think it's—"

"How do you know about that?" Carter asked, his focus sharp as a knife.

"How do *you* know about that?" she countered, stunned that Carter, who seemed so distanced from the family, would be aware of the gems.

"I know it was something Mom was messed up in a while back," Carter answered.

"Did she steal them from the original thief?"

"Maybe." Carter shrugged. "Who knows."

"Well, shouldn't we find out?"

"Why?" Carter asked, incredulous. He grabbed a jamjar glass from the cupboard and filled it with sweet tea from the pitcher at Savannah's elbow. "It's got nothing to do with us."

"What if someone is breaking into this house thinking we have the gems? And—" she put her hands on her hips, feeling suddenly as though he was treating her like the kid she'd stopped being years ago "—how do you know about the gems?"

Carter watched her for a long time then put down the glass. "Okay. But don't freak out."

"Spill, Carter."

"I was in touch with Mom ten years ago."

It was awful, the shock like ice. The pain like razors.

"Since then, I've had a private investigator checking up

on her once a year. He did some digging in the past and
came up with the Pacific Gems thing."

"Why didn't—" She swallowed. *Why didn't she come
back? Where is she? Why did she leave?* A thousand questions Savannah couldn't ask. "Why didn't you tell us?"

He blinked and looked away, hiding something. Carter
had a secret. Another one. Another mile in the distance
between her and her brothers. "Stop trying to protect me,"
she cried. "I'm not a kid."

"Our mother is not a nice woman," Carter said, his face
tight and hard.

"Carter, I know—"

"No, you don't. You don't remember the way she was.
You don't remember how she'd turn us on each other. How
she forgot about us."

"Okay, Carter," Savannah whispered, stunned to see
this sudden wrath. "I'm sorry."

He sighed, his shoulders so wide, so strong sagged
slightly. "No, I'm sorry. But whatever Mom is involved
in, she won't bring here. She knows better."

"But someone has already thought we know about those
gems, because of Mom's role in all this."

"Please, Savannah, don't worry about it. She's gone.
She's not coming back. Not now, not ever."

The way he said it sent chills across Savannah's skin,
little prickles that made the hair lift off her arms. "Why
do you sound so sure? She was in New Orleans, for crying
out loud. She was just a few hours away!"

The back door opened and Matt, sweaty and dark with
dirt, stepped in. Savannah's belly twisted and her body
burned at the sight of him. She went back to making sandwiches, praying Carter wouldn't notice.

"Sorry to interrupt," Matt said, lifting his thermos. "I
just wanted—"

"Matt Woods?" Carter asked, pushing away from the counter. He glanced wide-eyed at Savannah. "Your handyman is Matt Woods?"

Savannah nodded and Carter turned back to Matt, his mouth open, a thousand questions poised.

"I'll come back later," Matt said and ducked out the door.

"What is the Savior of the Inner City doing in your back courtyard?"

Savannah sighed. "Okay. But don't freak out."

THE CLOUDS WERE PINK in the west, dark in the east as Carter was leaving. Matt watched Savannah's brother hug Katie hard, swinging her slightly so the girl shrieked with laughter.

Savannah watched, her heart—wounded and bleeding—in her eyes.

Matt stood under the willow in the front yard, wishing he could put his arm around Savannah. Stand at her side and shore her up.

Carter was a good guy, even if he had trouble taking no for an answer. He'd come barreling out to the courtyard with lots of talk about the inner city of Baton Rouge and how it needed someone like Matt. Someone with vision.

Carter had talked about the old buildings, historical details falling to ruin and waste. Matt had actually salivated, his imagination shooting sparks.

Sparks he ruthlessly smothered.

"I'm not in the business of saving cities anymore," he'd said, keeping his head down, his hands busy.

"I understand. What happened in St. Louis must have been hard on you," Carter had said, digging in his wallet for a card. "But, if you change your mind."

They'd shaken hands, and before he'd returned to the

house Carter had apologized for his mother. "I'm sorry," he'd said. "For whatever role my mother might have had in your father's incarceration."

"My father knew the risks when he took those gems," Matt had said, slightly stunned that Carter felt the need to apologize for something so removed from him. "And really, outside of your mother, it doesn't seem to have anything to do with you or your family."

Carter had nodded then smiled, brilliant public figure once more. "I'll be hoping to hear from you. At least let me give you a tour of the city at some point."

"We'll see," Matt had said, when what he'd really wanted to say was *don't hold your breath.*

But now, Carter's business card vibrated in Matt's back pocket, making him wonder what he was going to do with himself once this courtyard was done. It would be soon—he'd finish planting the trees by tomorrow, the fountain would arrive on Wednesday, and he'd have to pick up some flowers and plants to fill in any leftover gaps.

Things were coming to an end here.

He couldn't return to St. Louis, to Steel and Wood Architecture, he knew that. He'd tie up some loose ends, make sure his existing contracts were dealt with, but there were too many memories there, not enough of them good.

Frankly, he wasn't sure he could ever design buildings again, and he didn't know where that left him. What would he love as much as he'd loved his work?

A hot breeze toyed with the fine hairs around Savannah's face as she leaned in to hug her brother.

"Christmas," she said.

"I can't promise," her brother agreed. "But I'll see what I can do about Tyler."

Katie cheered and Matt watched, his chest burning.

Matt's cell phone buzzed, startling him. He'd forgotten

he'd turned it on. Or even had it on him. Some kind of passive-aggressive flirtation with the life he'd left behind.

Nothing good would come of it, he was sure.

He opened it, braced for Erica, but got a surprise.

"You have a collect call from Martinsville Prison, do you accept the charges?"

Dad? He hadn't expected that. It wasn't even Wednesday.

"I do," he said and stepped deeper into the shadows.

"Matt?"

His father's tone, all *bon amie* and good times, made him smile. Good old Dad. It was nice to have something in his life that never changed.

"Hey, Dad."

"I tried you last Wednesday but—"

"I didn't have my phone on," he said. "I haven't until recently."

"Well, then, let me be the first to welcome you back to the living."

Matt smiled and ran his hands through his hair. *I need a haircut,* he realized. No doubt one of the many millions of things he needed to do when he was done with the courtyard.

"What's going on, Dad?"

"Well, I got an interesting visitor this morning."

"Not the stripper, again, she—"

"Richard Bonavie. He's back from the dead. Well, Los Angeles, actually, but I think that's a different story."

Matt sat down hard on the cement steps, feeling like his gut had turned to lead. The gems—he'd forgotten all about them. His whole reason for coming here, and they no longer mattered.

Not like Savannah.

He watched her, the sun in her hair, a smile on her face.

So much had changed, so much was different, and he didn't care anymore, about the gems, the theft. A month ago, he'd been determined to get justice, but now this information left him cold. Sad, even. Sad that his father was who he was. The kind of man who'd been lured into a scheme that was way over his head then had gotten burned.

Matt heard the scratch and flicker of a lighter and his father took a deep breath and exhaled, smoke no doubt a cloud around his head. "You won't believe what Richard—"

"Dad." Matt sighed. His father was excited, juiced up about whatever this news was, and Matt wished there was a way to tell him he wasn't interested without hurting Joel's feelings. "I don't want to know."

"What?"

"I don't want to know. I can't fix this for you, Dad. I can't...I'm sorry."

"Son." His father's voice was warm and Matt put his hand against the tree, wishing there weren't miles and steel bars between them. "You've got nothing to be sorry for."

"Yeah, but I got your hopes up—"

"My hopes?" Dad laughed. "I'm out in six months for a crime I committed. Finding out where Vanessa and Richard are or what they did that night wouldn't change that."

"Then why...?" Matt trailed off, a big chasm closing in his head, his chest. He knew why his father sent him here—the answer was in his past. "Remember when I was a kid and you'd take me to those casinos?"

"I've already apologized for that, Matt. I can't change the mistakes I made."

"I know, but remember that game, the man with the scar and the patch and the hat?"

There was a long pause and finally his dad said, "Yes, I remember."

"Why'd you do that?"

"Because you were scared. Because you were bored. Because you've got a real big brain, son, and without something to occupy it, you'd go crazy."

Matt leaned back, looked up at the bright blue sky. "That's why you told me about Vanessa and Richard."

"You were so lost, son, after that accident. I couldn't stand watching you fade away like that. I was losing you, and I knew that if I could get you interested in something again, anything, you'd find your way back."

Matt squinted at the horizon, feeling emotion bite hard at the back of his eyes. "Thank you, Dad."

"I can only guess that you've figured out that clearing my dirty name isn't going to change what happened in St. Louis."

Nothing would bring back Peter. Or fix the lives of all the people affected by the collapse. Nothing would stop the occasional nightmare that woke Matt shaking and screaming in the night.

"I'm working on it," he finally answered.

"Look, I know I haven't been an ideal father—"

Matt snorted.

"But I care about you, I always have. I'm glad you're putting it behind you."

Matt's heart flexed and stuttered. He couldn't argue. For all his father's many faults, not caring about Matt was not one of them. Joel wouldn't win any father of the year awards, but he'd been there. At least there had been Rachmaninoff and card games and dinners and warm beds.

"I know, Dad," Matt said, his voice gruff.

"Good. Then tell me, when I'm out, where are you going to be?"

"I think," he said, feeling the words roll up from his gut like stones, filling his mouth until he had to spit them out. "I think I have to go back to St. Louis to tie up some loose ends."

There was a commotion on Joel's side of the line. "Uh-oh," he said. "Looks like Little Adam got some bad news from his wife. They're going to clear us out of here, son."

"Dad," Matt said. "Is everything okay, though? That Richard visit—was there something wrong? Something I should know?"

Joel took another long drag from his cigarette and Matt waited, nervous for some reason.

"Don't worry about it, Matt," Joel said. "It was nothing."

"You're sure?"

"Absolutely."

"Talk to you in a few days," Matt said and hung up.

He couldn't fix Savannah and the mess he'd made here, he couldn't fix his father's crime—the only thing he could fix was his own life.

And it was time he did it.

Before he could curb the impulse, he dialed his office number. It was late on Sunday so he left a message that Erica would get in the morning.

"I'm sorry," he said. "I owe you." He paused. "I owe you so much, Erica." He did some quick math, figured out how many days work he had left.

"I'll be back next Monday," he said. "I promise. I know that might not mean much right now, and if you want to leave I don't blame you, but I will be back in town in a week to clear things up."

He shut his phone, wondering if he'd done the right

thing. Stepping back into the land of the living was not something he could undo.

Giving himself a deadline to leave the Manor and Savannah was something he could not undo. He'd have to leave on Sunday to be in St. Louis on Monday.

Which gave him seven days.

Carter's car started and drove away, spitting gravel as it went. Matt turned and there was Savannah, Katie scowling at her side.

Savannah's eyes searched his face, just as he searched hers, trying to read her emotions on her skin.

"You okay?" she asked.

"I don't know," he said. "You?"

She shook her head, tears welling in her eyes, and he wished there was something he could do. Something that would help.

Then she stepped up against him, her body flush to his and her arms slid around his back, her fingers lighting fires through his shirt, holding him close. Tight.

Breath left his body in a gust and his hands trailed up her back, to her shoulders, feeling the skin and muscle of her arms and neck. So strong, this woman.

He pressed his cheek to the top of her head, getting drunk on the smell of flowers and dried sweat in her hair.

Electricity fired through his body but he ignored it.

Ignored the snarling desire for more of her.

It was only a hug. Comfort.

Where he least expected it and wanted it most.

Seven days, he thought. And swore.

MONDAY MORNING, Savannah climbed the stone steps to the Bonne Terre Library and unlocked its heavy wooden doors. Inside, the cool, still air smelled like books, wood cleaner and damp from the basement that had never dried out from Hurricane Katrina.

"Lucy!" she said with her best Desi impression, "I'm home."

She got to work, occupying herself with the piles of tasks that had accumulated in her absence. She was grateful for the distraction, but even with the work, Matt was there. Lingering in the corners of her mind, he was never far from any thought she had.

He was different. Changed. He might not be able to see it, but she could. She felt it in that hug last night—the way he'd let himself be touched.

She wished, stupidly, that his letting go of his grief and guilt might mean something for her.

Like he'd stick around.

But he wouldn't. No one ever did.

By noon, the air conditioner was battling the humidity that pressed down from outside and the summer school kids were at the computers.

Including Garrett and Owen.

Looking at them, her blood literally boiled. Two weeks since the first break-in and there they were, as if nothing had ever happened. She had to drink a big glass of cold water to stop herself from incinerating.

She reconsidered her thoughts of revenge—maybe that letter to their parents? But it didn't seem like enough. Nothing seemed like enough.

"Hot one today, huh?" Janice, her assistant, asked. They stood at the sink, Janice filling up the WeightWatchers water bottle she kept at her desk—along with the Fannie May sampler box she didn't think anyone knew about.

"Hey," Savannah said, turning sideways and resting her hip against the counter. "So what's happening with the love triangle out there?"

"Well." Janice nearly shook with sudden excitement and the cats on her pink T-shirt struggled to stay on her mountainous breasts. "I caught Garrett and The Cheerleader kissing down by the drinking fountains."

"Does Owen know?"

"Not at all." Janice shook her head, her eyes twinkling.

Savannah, as she had since the moment she'd hired Janice, felt like hugging the woman.

"Why?" Janice asked. "You suddenly interested in the love lives of summer school students?"

Savannah shrugged, heading to the front desk and the stacks of mail she needed to go through. "No reason."

But Matt's words hummed through her bloodstream. *Guilt deserves to be punished.*

While she was convinced the adage no longer applied to Matt, it sure as hell applied to the two kids smirking at her over their computer screens.

She shrugged off the chains she kept around those O'Neill impulses and when she finally saw Owen's girlfriend head for the bathroom, Garrett not far behind her, she strolled up to Owen.

"I need to do some maintenance on that computer," she said. "Why don't you take a bathroom break?"

"Whatever," he said and took off for the stairs. And, Savannah could only hope, a very ugly surprise.

Savannah smirked.

"Savannah?" Janice said from the front desk, holding the phone. "It's a man named Matt for you. He says he can't find Katie."

"DID YOU CHECK in the tree?" Savannah demanded as she came charging through the door. He'd expected her to come running, but the anger was a surprise.

"Of course," he said. "When the water balloons didn't come at noon that was the first place I checked."

"Where's Margot?" she snapped and threw her purse down on the kitchen counter. She was back in her prison warden outfit, all straight lines and buttons, but her hair was loose, pulled away from her face with a headband. A variation on her theme.

Her beauty and all those buttons totally wrecked him.

He coughed and stepped behind the counter so she wouldn't notice his totally inappropriate erection.

"Right here," Margot said, stepping into the kitchen wearing her robe.

"Good lord, Margot," Savannah said. "It's past noon and you're just getting up?"

"So it would seem." Margot's eyes twinkled as she crossed to the coffeepot.

"Where have you been?"

"Anthony took me to New Orleans for the weekend. I got home late last night." She filled a china teacup with coffee and sipped it black. "What's got you in an uproar this morning?"

"Katie's gone," Matt said.

Margot blinked and turned to Savannah. "Gone?"

"No one's seen her today. God, I hope she's just hiding," Savannah said. "This is what she usually does." Turning back to Margot, she said, "I heard you come in last night, and I figured you'd keep an eye on her."

"I'm sorry," Margot said. "I forgot you went to work today. She just got—"

"Lost in the shuffle." Savannah's anger vanished and she looked so guilt-stricken it made Matt's stomach do a flip. "She's so mad at me right now. Did you check the rosebush or the kud—" She stopped and swore. "They're all gone. All her hiding spots."

She bent her head back so she could stare up at the ceiling and feel terrible about herself.

He wanted to hug her, ease that stress the way she'd eased his last night. The way she hugged him as if she cared, as if she saw right through to the bone and heart and blood that he was made up of, to the hard kernel that remained from the accident, like scar tissue.

"I'll look upstairs," Margot said, putting down her cup.

"I'll check my office."

The women were gone, leaving behind their individual scents, lemon and roses and the slightly acrid tang of regret and worry.

Matt didn't know how he could help, or if his help would be accepted, but he wanted to do something. Wished he could do something. Anything. For her.

Savannah came barreling into the kitchen.

"No sign of her?" he asked.

"She's not in the office," Savannah said, grim and stony-faced. "Did you check the sleeping porch?"

"No," he said. "Why do you think she'd go there?"

"She's eight and she's mad, Matt. Who knows why she's doing anything?"

It was a good point and Matt stepped into her wake, following her to his room.

SAVANNAH OPENED the big wood-and-glass doors to the sleeping porch and listened for any signs of her runaway daughter.

"I know you're in here," she said, opening a closet in the corner. Nothing but a long forgotten winter coat and a dusty Christmas wreath.

Guilt was a stitch in her side as she scanned the nearly empty room. Only Matt's neatly made bed and duffel bag.

The terra cotta flowerpots, cracked and covered in dust, sat in the corner.

The smell of him—sunshine and hard work and something clean, something totally Matt—was everywhere.

She'd forgotten her daughter today. Forgotten her. And she wasn't stupid. She knew, in part, it was because of Matt, because of this growing obsession she had with not only the Elements Building tragedy.

But with him.

Did good mothers forsake their attraction to men for their kids? Was that what was required of her right now?

Because she didn't want to let go of it. Even though she knew Matt was leaving, she wanted something of the time he was here.

A taste of him.

Clearly, she was the worst mother in the world. But she wasn't going to apologize. A few months ago, she would have, she would have turned her back on what she wanted, but she was different now.

Matt Woods stepping into her life had changed her.

"I know you're mad," she said to her daughter as if she could see her. She got down on her knees and looked under the bed. At first, nothing but dust bunnies the size of her head then, at the foot, her daughter's defiant blue eyes.

"Katie." She sighed, holding out her hands, reaching for her daughter's outstretched palm.

"I've been here for like, three hours!" Katie yelled. "I'm stuck."

Savannah smiled, though she felt like crying, and pulled Katie from where she was wedged on her side under the bed, her legs curled up to her pointy little chin.

"My legs don't work right," Katie muttered, sticking her face into Savannah's neck. Savannah fell back on her butt and cradled her daughter close.

"They're asleep," she said. "Give them a few minutes."
She pulled dust bunnies and cobwebs from Katie's hair and
brushed the worst of the mess off the second set of Asian
pajamas from Margot's cruise. Ruined, of course.

"I'm really sorry about today," she murmured into the
pink shell of Katie's ear.

Katie pulled back, her eyes accusing her of everything
short of a third world war. "You just left."

"I thought Margot was watching you."

"You left me here with—" Katie's eyes flickered over
Savannah's shoulder and went cold and hard "—that
guy."

Savannah felt Matt over her shoulder, a warm solid
weight like a hand against her skin. She wanted to laugh at
the thought of Matt as just *that guy.* Somehow, someway,
in the past few weeks, he'd become far more than that.

What he was, however, she couldn't be sure.

"Matt is not *that guy,*" Savannah said, trying to be
patient.

"Then who is he?" Katie asked. She shook, her eyes
direct, her hands in fists, and Savannah wondered if this
was more than jealousy over the amount of time and attention she'd been giving to Matt.

Savannah darted a quick glance at Matt, who was as
baffled as she was and as conflicted about her as she was
about him. It was right there, easy to read in the set of his
shoulders, the lines in the corner of his mouth. "He's a
friend," she said, perhaps more to him than Katie.

"Is he my dad?"

CHAPTER FOURTEEN

SAVANNAH STARED BLANKLY at Katie, her head trying to catch up with what just happened.

"Your dad?" she asked. "Why in the world would you think that?"

Katie's little chin came up. "That day outside the library you and Margot were talking about my dad and then Matt said you guys were talking about him. And then he made you cry and you wouldn't answer me when I asked if you had sex with him."

All of that was true, Savannah thought, but it was like adding apples and oranges and getting elephants.

"Honey," she breathed. "I had no idea you were thinking this."

"You never tell me anything," Katie said.

"I thought I was protecting you," she said. The same way Carter always tried to protect her from the uglier aspects of Tyler or their mother.

She felt awful that she'd never seen the pain not talking about Eric was causing Katie. Other single mothers probably didn't have this problem. They probably told their kids the truth from the beginning and—rubbing salt in her guilt—she imagined they were able to do it without calling the absent father a bastard.

"Marybeth, at school," Katie said, "she doesn't have a dad but her mom told her he lives in New Orleans with a hooker."

Savannah swallowed her laughter—clearly there was a spectrum of bad single parenting.

"But she gets to go visit him," Katie continued, getting worked up. "They eat beignets for dinner and I don't even know where my dad is. And then when you came—" she looked at Matt then shrugged "—everybody got so weird."

Matt stepped past Savannah and collapsed on the bed as though his knees had just been broken. "I'm not your father, Katie," he whispered, his green eyes sincere and earnest in a million different ways.

"You're not?" she asked, and he shook his head. "You're sure?"

"Very sure. If I was your father, I would have been here your whole life," he said. Katie's chin dropped a notch, and Savannah's whole body started to shake. "I never would have left you."

Savannah could not look Matt in the eyes. Actually, she really could barely stand to be in the same room as him, the embodiment of everything she refused to want but wanted anyway.

Katie's blue eyes pierced her, lanced her right through the throat, and every decision she'd made over the years to run from this conversation came home to roost.

Savannah took a deep breath and stepped right over the dark, bottomless, treacherous cavern that was the who is your father conversation. The conversation that she'd feared and dreaded and run away from. The conversation that she'd put off time and time again, thinking she'd get to it when Katie was older or when she asked.

That time was now. Actually the time was probably years ago.

"I'm going to let you guys talk," Matt said. His gaze brushed Savannah's then clung as time froze to a halt.

Funny how she'd thought she could fall in love with Matt Howe, but it was nothing compared to what she was capable of feeling for Matt Woods.

Matt cleared his throat and broke eye contact, crouching in front of Katie, his gaze serious. "Wherever your dad is," he said, "he's missing out on a great girl."

He stood, his fingers brushing Savannah's shoulder, sending flashes of heat and pulses of light through her entire body, as he left.

Savannah took a second to pull in all the ragged edges and loose ends and compose herself.

Here we go.

"Your father," Savannah finally said, hugging her daughter close, "is a man named Eric Carlyse."

THE TREES WERE PLANTED, the saplings' tender branches and bright new green leaves swayed in the late afternoon breeze. Without much growth the pattern of the maze was pretty clear, but in a few years when the trees were mature…Matt smiled. Well, then it would perfect. Nooks and crannies. Dead ends. Hidey-holes. The maze, though small, had it all.

Matt couldn't even begin to imagine all the trouble a girl like Katie could get into with this in her backyard.

It would be something to see. Something he'd like to see.

Lifting his arm, he scratched at the worst of the grit and dirt that clung to his neck and face. He needed a shower and a change of clothes, but as far as he knew, Katie and Savannah were still planted in his room.

Man, what a weird day. He didn't like seeing those girls so hurt, wished he knew a better way to help than to step aside and build a maze.

Katie needed a father. In fact, thinking about the falling apart O'Neill house of estrogen, and that hot and hungry look Savannah had in her eyes when she watched him working—to be totally caveman about it—a man was needed by all of them.

The door opened and shut and he turned to find Katie standing in the sparkly bright light that signaled the end of the day. Her eyes were red-rimmed and her cheeks flushed, but she wasn't bristling with anger.

"Hi," he said, cautiously.

"Hi." She scratched at her knee, then her elbow. "I'm supposed to apologize for being mean to you."

Ah.

"Understandable," he said, "considering who you thought I was."

"I'm sorry about the water balloons."

"Forgiven," he said with a quick nod. "You okay?"

Katie pursed her lips as if she were weighing her answer. "Sure." But she sighed and plunked her hands on her hips. "My dad is a jerk. He has a bunch of other kids in Chicago."

"Wow."

"He never told Mom and she never told me because she didn't want me to get hurt."

"Makes sense, I guess," he said.

Matt sat on the step and pulled off his gloves. Katie jumped from the landing with both feet and sat beside him. "It's his loss, you know," Matt said and Katie looked at him out of the corner of her eye. "I mean, I'm sure those other kids are fine, but they're not you."

Katie blinked down at her fingers, twisting them into knots as if playing some kind of game. Sadness dripped off her like bitter honey.

"I bet," he said, "they don't know card tricks. Or how to play poker. They probably can't climb trees like you can. I'm sure they can't hide as well as you can."

She smiled, sadly, but didn't look up.

"They don't make your mom happy like you do," he said.

"You make my mom happy," she said. "Now, I mean—not before. Before you made her cry, but now you make her happy. I can tell."

Only an idiot would misread the hope in that little girl's face. And he was no idiot.

"I'm leaving on Sunday, when I'm done with the courtyard," he said, softly, carefully, not wanting to cause this little girl any more pain. "I can't stay here."

"Where do you have to go?" Katie asked.

"Back to St. Louis," he said, wondering why the words stuck and filled his mouth. Wondering why the future looked so damn bleak. "I have a lot of things I need to fix up there."

Katie twisted her lips. "Well, when you're done with that you should come back," she said and jumped to her feet. As if it was that simple.

Man, you gotta love kids, he thought, *they rebounded so fast.* All that sadness was gone, at least for the time being.

On the other hand, he knew he would never rebound from his time spent here. Not in a million years. He didn't even want to try.

"Remember what you said the other day about teaching me how you beat me at poker?" she asked.

He smiled. "I do."

"How about tonight?"

"You're on."

MIDNIGHT FOUND MATT back in the good graces of Margot and Katie. He sat, a scotch at his elbow, one of Margot's fine cigars between his lips.

Like a stranger brought in out of the cold and propped in front of a fire, Matt stretched out his legs and luxuriated in the moment.

He totally understood, right now, why his father had loved the tables so much. Why he'd sat again and again with the last of his money, with his kid waiting outside in the car—because it was warm.

Friendly, when the world was upside down.

"Katie," he said, getting on with his lesson. "I hate to break it to you, but you've got a tell."

Katie gasped as if he'd offended her honor. "I do not!"

"You do." He leaned forward and caught Margot's smile out of the corner of his eye. "When you've got a good hand you sit really, really still." Katie's eyes went wide as understanding dawned. "The rest of the time you're like a jumping bean."

"Oh, my gosh!" she breathed, then looked to Margot for confirmation.

"The man is right," Margot said. "The more still and quiet you get, the better your hand."

"So," she asked wide-eyed, "what do I do?"

"Sit still!" Margot cried. "All the time. It's what your mother and I have been telling you for years."

The door behind Matt slid open, letting in a draft and the distinctive fragrance of lemon and vanilla. Katie's eyes went wide, the cards fluttered out of her hands onto the table.

Margot swore.

Busted. Very, very busted.

"So," Savannah said. "Here's where you all are."

"Hello, Savannah," Matt said, turning to see her in the doorway, her arms crossed over the robe that was quickly becoming his favorite piece of clothing on the planet.

"What's happening here?" she asked, ignoring him. He thought it was fairly obvious—Margot practically looked like a Vegas dealer with the deck of cards in her hand.

But when his companions stayed silent, Matt took the bull by the horns.

"Just a friendly game of poker," Matt said.

"Matt!" Katie snapped. "What are you doing?"

"Like she doesn't know?" he asked. "I'm pretty sure we're all busted."

"Let me guess," Savannah said, addressing her daughter. "Matt's teaching you poker? Like he taught you those card tricks?"

"No," Katie admitted, pushing the cards away.

"Don't be angry, Savannah," Margot said.

"Angry?" Savannah asked. Matt winced at the tone of her voice, scooting his chair to the side in case fire shot out of her eyes. "Why would I be angry? I've only asked that this sort of behavior stop and that Katie, my eight-year-old, not learn how to gamble!"

"We're not gambling," Margot replied. "There are no stakes. She wanted to learn, Savannah. She's been doing those card tricks for years and she's so bright. She's really very good." Savannah's eyes flared and Margot shut up, looking as contrite as a woman could, drinking a glass of scotch and smoking a cigar.

"It's only bad if you let it be," Matt said.

"What do you know about it?" Savannah snapped.

"I know that my dad used to leave me in the car so he could play blackjack. I know that after my mom died we had to move four times in the middle of the night because he'd lost the rent money. I know that when the cards went his way I got to eat steak and shrimp and drink Cherry Coke out of fancy glasses, and when they didn't, I ate macaroni and cheese."

Savannah licked her lips, leaving them damp and pink and he tried hard not to be distracted.

"But he always fed me. There was always a warm place to sleep. He helped me with my homework and was there for me. And I know he tried, Savannah. He really tried. And it took a long time, but I forgave him for those nights out in the car and the macaroni and cheese."

"What's wrong with macaroni and cheese?" Katie asked and Matt smiled at her. Really, she was such a cool kid.

"Nothing, but when you eat it for breakfast, lunch and dinner for, like, three weeks in a row it gets pretty gross."

Katie nodded in sage agreement and he looked back at Savannah.

"I spent a long time trying to rise above my roots," he said, remembering what Margot and Katie had said about Savannah the first time they'd played cards. "But it got easier to just live with them."

Savannah's eyes flashed to Margot who shrugged, delicately. "The man is right. You're an O'Neill, and so is your daughter. No use pretending otherwise."

"Stay," Matt pleaded, his eyes on Savannah. Katie beside him lit up like a skyrocket was inside of her.

"Yeah, Mom, stay."

"Stay and have some fun."

"Fun?" Savannah asked, as if she were considering eating poison.

Matt, Katie and Margot all nodded and pulled up a chair from the corner, pushing a shopping bag off its seat.

"Stay," he said.

He could see the weigh scales inside of her head, the

intricate systems she used to balance what she was against what she thought she and her whole family should be. He saw it all and he waited, hoping she could stop torturing herself with the idea of being someone else, and simply be happy with who she was.

She jerked the tie on her robe tighter and stepped to the table, all business.

"What are we playing?" she asked and everyone cheered.

And Matt fell totally in love.

TWO HOURS LATER Katie was curled up on Margot's bed and Matt was getting schooled.

"You've got to be kidding me," he said, watching as Savannah laid down her flush, killing his two of a kind. For about the third time in a row.

"She always was the best card player," Margot said, watching her granddaughter with pride. "Even better than Tyler."

Savannah's smile was like a kitten with its paw in the cream, and it went right into his bloodstream. The robe's tie was giving up the fight and shadows lingered between her breasts, the plush white curves of which looked like velvet against the dark satin robe.

She was all contradiction right now. Light and dark. Serious and coy. Flirtatious and crushing all in the same glance. Those breasts, her diamond-bright eyes, her long fingers, the swell and dip of her lips as she tried not to smile.

Her hair, all that magnificent blond hair, like some kind of veil.

And she was a shark. An absolute card-playing shark. He was in love. No doubt about it. After she'd spanked him in the second hand he looked up into her laughing blue eyes and realized—this was it.

There would never be another woman for him.

"You're not too bad yourself," Savannah said, watching him from the corner of her eye, a smile on her lips.

Christ, his erection pounded under the table. Absolutely all his blood was in his lap. He could barely see straight.

"I should go," he said, after counting to a hundred and thinking of trees and sod and seedlings and anything but his disastrous feelings for Savannah.

"Me, too," Savannah said, pushing the cards to the center of the table. She looked into the shadows where Katie was sound asleep on Margot's king-size bed.

"Leave her," Margot said. "No point in waking her now."

Savannah nodded and stood. Realizing how loose her robe was, she tightened it, a blush on her creamy cheeks.

Sod. Rocks. Plants. Hard work.

He walked with her to the hallway, his blood still pounding, his mind crowded with thoughts of her, both imagined and real of her.

"Did you want to…" She stopped in front of the library where the baby grand gleamed in the moonlight. She turned toward him, so close he could smell her, so close he could see her pulse in her throat, and he lost control of his impulses. His feelings for her flooded the dam and he was powerless against them.

He cradled her face in his hands and kissed her.

CHAPTER FIFTEEN

HE EXPECTED A SLAP, a push, some kind of violent rejection, and he waited, absorbing the feel of her lips against his before she shoved him away.

But it didn't come.

She was all taut and trembling muscle, then the heavens opened, a chorus of angels sang and she kissed him back.

Throwing her arms around his neck she knocked him backward and he collided with the wall. He hauled her close and high against his body, taking her weight in his arms, pressing her hard against every part of himself.

She arched her hips against his, her teeth bit into his lips and he growled, low and menacing, feeling so close to out of control he was freaked.

"Savannah," he said, between long sucking bites at her mouth. Her lips tasted like honey and inside... He groaned, sinking into her. "We have to stop."

"Why?" she sighed, reaching those beloved hands up his shirt and across the hard muscles of his stomach that jumped in appreciation.

More. Oh, man, he wanted so much more with her. He wanted everything. He wanted to push her against the wall and eat her. He wanted to lay her out on a bed and cherish her, love her, and at the same time he wanted to bend her over a chair and make her scream as she came.

"It's a now or never type thing," he finally managed

to say, forcing himself not to shove his thigh between her legs.

She pulled back, her fingers still drawing little circles over his skin. Torture. She was killing him with those circles.

"I've wanted you since the moment I saw you," he said, watching the truth sink into those blue eyes, lighting them up from deep inside. "And, as much as I'd like to pretend I've got rock-solid control, I don't. Not around you. So, we should stop."

Her lips pursed and he had to put his hands against the wall or that robe would not live another day.

"I don't want to stop," she said. Those circles under his shirt grew and grew until one of her blunt nails raked across his nipple.

"I have to leave on Sunday," he said. "I…can't stay."

I could come back, he thought, but didn't say. *One word from you and I would be back here like a boomerang.*

"I know," she said, her smile ghostly. "But I want this," she whispered, leaning up to kiss him, her teeth taking a small bite out of his lip. "I want everything you have to give me. For however long I can have it."

"Savannah," he groaned, her name a plea. It occurred to him to ask if she was sure, but then her hand slid down the front of his pants.

Doesn't get more sure than that.

He swept her up in his arms, feeling very Rhett Butler.

Using his foot, he bumped open the door to the sleeping porch.

As she slid down onto the bed like bourbon out of a bottle, the look in her eyes was a challenge and his blood pounded in response. Savannah wanted sex. And as she leaned backward and spread herself out against the faded, soft sheets, her knees bent, her arms spread, the tie on her robe giving up the best of her secrets, he knew how she wanted it.

The same way he did.

Wild. Hot. Now.

He leaned down and pushed open her robe, revealing the perfection of her body. The tight curve of her breast, the taut belly, the gorgeous mystery at the apex of her thighs.

Her skin was silk under his hand, her nipples hard as he rolled them against his palm, pinched them, just enough that her eyes went hazy, her lips parted in a moan.

He licked her open mouth, toying with her lips, her tongue, until she pushed herself up and sealed her mouth to his.

Then the fun really started.

His clothes, barely touched by her long elegant hands, fell off his body until they were skin to skin. The electrical current between them could light up the Manor for months, years.

She was strong and her muscles held him tight, gripped him hard. A leg around his hip, an arm around his shoulders and it felt as though she might never let him go.

And that was so okay with him.

His erection brushed the liquid heat between her legs and they both gasped, arching hard into each other.

"You better have protection," she whispered into his ear, licking the rim, biting the lobe and his brain went blank.

Protection?

Her fingertips danced over his erection, her thumb tracing circles around the head. "Condom?" she said.

He blinked, unable to tell whether she was speaking English.

"Matt?" She smiled, womanly and knowing.

"You're killing me," he breathed, closing his eyes when both her hands got in on the act.

"We'll both be hurting if you don't have a condom."

Oh, right. A condom.

He kissed her hard and leaned up on his arms, reluctant to leave the stunning heat of her body. More so when her breasts were gilded in moonlight, the nipples dark and hard. He sucked one into his mouth, grazing it with his teeth.

"A condom!" she cried, pushing him away slightly. "Hurry."

He leaped from the bed and found his kit bag, grateful he hadn't emptied it since his ski trip with Pauline almost a year ago. He pulled out a ribbon of condoms and whirled back to the bed.

Man, she was beautiful. Long-limbed and naked, her eyes hot, her lips wet.

"You're staring, Matt," she murmured, her legs falling open slightly, an erotic invitation.

"I'm stunned, Savannah," he said, suddenly humbled that all this was even happening.

I love you. He caught the words in time, shoving away the impulse to tell her how he felt. It seemed wrong to do it now, as if all that he was feeling was tied to sex, which couldn't be further from the truth. When he told her—if he told her—he wanted her to know it as the truth.

He'd come here looking for justice and found something better.

Salvation.

"You okay?" she asked, tilting her head. All that hair, silver in the moonlight, fell over her shoulder, and he couldn't have walked away from her if he was on fire. There was simply no way.

"You're a goddess," he said. Her answering smile was

indulgent, doubtful, and he knew that she didn't believe him. Didn't see all of her own beauty.

"And you're very far away." She smiled. "Come back to bed."

He crawled over her body, pressing kisses to her knees, blowing air into the damp curls between her thighs, licking her belly button.

"You don't believe me?" he asked, stroking the hair from her face.

"About what?" she panted, arching herself against the leg he pressed between hers. He pushed harder against her and she groaned, grinding herself against him.

"That you're a goddess."

"I have nice hair," she conceded.

Laughter gushed out of him. "You're stunning. Every inch of you."

"Matt." She shook her head. Her modesty doubled his lust. She didn't know. She had no idea.

I'm going to have to show her.

His blood pounded and his mouth watered at the thought.

Retracing his steps, he trailed his tongue along those stunning collarbones, kissed his way across her breasts. Found every rib with his lips.

A kiss on her belly button and he slid down, easing open her thighs.

"Matt," she sighed, pushing her fingers into his hair, scratching and petting him as he made his way to her secret heart and settled in to make love to the damp, hot mystery that was Savannah O'Neill.

SAVANNAH CALLED IN SICK the next day for the first time since Katie had gotten the chicken pox when she was a year old.

"You can handle things there, Janice," Savannah said.

"Well, sure I can," Janice agreed. "I'm just surprised is all. You don't sound too sick."

"It's a stomach thing," Savannah said and shot Matt a dirty look while he pressed kisses to the trembling skin of her belly. His chuckle blew hot air across incredibly sensitive flesh.

"I…ah…gotta go, Janice. I'll talk to you soon." She hung up Matt's cell phone and glared at him, his rumpled hair so dark against her and the white sheets. His eyes so green, his smile so warm.

A knot of something hard and sad sat in her throat and she swallowed past it, not wanting sadness. Not now. Not until the moment Matt walked away. Until then, she wanted to absorb every single ounce and fleck of joy she could.

"You're in trouble," she told him, laughing as he tickled her belly button with his tongue. She kicked her leg over him and rolled him to his back.

The condoms, two fewer than before, were in reach and she tore another one from the strip.

"No," Matt joked, palming her breasts. "Not that. Anything but that."

She slid the condom on him, her fingers running over him until he groaned, his hands digging into her skin.

They were both covered in little bruises and marks, physical proof of how out of control they'd gotten last night.

Proof of how out of control she was.

This is going to hurt, she told herself. *When he leaves it's going to hurt like nothing ever has.*

But she didn't care. She'd take the pain later if it ensured the pleasure now. Because right now, she felt as though she'd die without the pleasure.

"I'm afraid so," she said, using her best librarian

voice and his eyes flared. "You've been very bad, Matt Woods."

"Yeah?" He groaned and she slid down on him, until she could feel him in her heart. He rocked upward, and she moaned, sitting back on him, her thoughts scattering. "How bad can you be, Savannah?" he asked, his voice like honey.

She leaned down over him, her breasts against his hot chest, her tongue licking at his mouth. "Put on your glasses," she said. "And I'll show you."

"YOU CALLING IN SICK AGAIN?" Margot asked on Friday, as they waited for the coffee to brew.

Savannah nodded and cleared her throat, careful not to look at Margot, or let her look too closely at her. "Stomach thing," she said, cupping her coffee mug to her chest like a secret.

"That's a whole week."

"It's a bad stomach thing," she said, biting out the words. She knew down to the minute how much time she had left with Matt.

Matt chose that moment to step out of the sleeping porch carrying his thermos, looking to her like a man who'd been gorging on sex.

"Morning," he said into the silence.

"Matt," Margot said knowingly, her eyes sliding to Savannah.

Savannah yanked the coffeepot free, spilling coffee over her hand.

"Hello, Savannah," Matt said, his voice rich with laughter as though he knew she was ready to die from embarrassment. He pressed a kiss to the side of her head, patted her waist and headed out the door to the back courtyard, whistling as he went.

"Seems to me," Margot said, taking the pot from Savannah's death grip, "you have a Matt thing."

"I have a..." Savannah paused, not sure how to finish that sentence. *Heartache coming? Hole in my head?* "None of your business."

"I was right, wasn't I?" Margot asked, leaning one hip against the counter. "You like him."

Savannah didn't say anything. Of course she liked him, an idiot could see that. An idiot could probably see that she was dangerously close to being in love with him.

"You told Katie about her father?" Margot asked.

"I did. It was time—she'd started to think that Matt was her father." Margot's jaw dropped open. "I know." Savannah managed to laugh a little. "But with me never telling her anything, she started to answer her own questions. Matt got caught in the crossfire."

"He's very good with her," Margot said.

Savannah lifted her eyes to see Matt and Katie in the back courtyard. He was carrying a huge, burlap-wrapped bundle, every muscle straining against his shirt.

Katie leaped and danced around him like a muddy, tangle-haired butterfly.

"That man is good for you," Margot whispered. "That man is good for both of you. You're changing because of him."

It was true. More than true. There were parts of herself she didn't recognize. Every morning she looked in the mirror expecting to see that she'd become a redhead, or grown a third eye, or something dramatic that would match the utter transformation happening in her heart.

"It doesn't matter," Savannah said, tears in the back of her throat, "whether I like him or not. Whether he's good for us or not. Whether I'm changing or whatever. He has to leave on Sunday."

"You could go with him."

"Please," she scoffed.

"You think he won't ask? That man looks at you like you've buttered his bread."

"I have," she snapped. "But that doesn't mean anything. You know that better than anyone."

Margot arched an eyebrow. "Don't be catty," she said. "He looks at you like you matter. Like you're important to him."

Savannah took small sips of air, feeling as though the whole world was just too tight. In bed with him, his arm around her waist, his breath on her neck, anything seemed possible. It seemed possible that he might stay. That he might love her.

But when she got out of bed and walked around the house where her family had left her, a space opened up in her chest and doubt settled in. Reality fell around her like a hailstorm.

"He came here for his father and he's staying out of guilt for having lied," she said, not entirely convinced of that but unsure of what she should believe. "He's got me all wrapped up in this building collapse thing."

"You don't really believe that, do you?"

"I do," she said emphatically, convincing herself at the same time. "He'll leave here, get back to his life and forget all about me."

"Well, of course he will if you let him go without a fight."

"A fight?" Savannah asked, laughing at the truly ridiculous idea. "How?"

"Go with him," Margot said, grabbing Savannah's arms and giving her a little shake. "There's a world out there. A big one. And instead of looking at it through your computer, you should try to experience some of it."

The back door creaked open and Matt stuck his head in, his smile so pure it stabbed right through her. "Hate to break up the conversation, but Katie is getting anxious to get this fountain in place."

Savannah nodded, tugging herself free from Margot's gentle grip.

Today was fountain day. Tomorrow Matt would do the last of the flower planting and sometime tomorrow afternoon their new courtyard would be revealed.

And on Sunday, Matt would leave. Get in his car and drive away.

Monday was a mystery, a great gaping hole that was tearing her into pieces.

"I'm going to help Matt in the backyard." She practically threw her mug into the sink, her untouched coffee sloshing over the cream ceramic.

Avoiding her grandmother's eyes, she wished with her whole body and everything in her heart that she was back in bed with Matt, his arm a solid weight around her waist making everything as it was supposed to be.

CHAPTER SIXTEEN

KATIE AND SAVANNAH STOOD BACK, shovels in hand, and considered fountain positioning while Matt struggled under the weight of the enormous, burlap-covered object.

"It would help if we knew what the fountain was," Katie said. "If it's a butterfly…"

Matt, arms straining, muscles burning, tried very hard not to snap at them to make up their damn minds. "It's not a butterfly," he grunted.

"A unicorn?"

"Sorry."

"Whatever it is," Savannah said, "I think the center of the maze is perfect."

Thank you, he thought, letting the fountain rest on the earth.

"You like it there?" Katie asked. "Really?"

"Yeah." Savannah tilted her head to the side. "I do."

"You've got two choices, ladies," Matt said. "The plumbing only works here or next to the house. Take your pick."

Savannah and Katie shared a cryptic look, and now that his muscles weren't about to snap he could appreciate what a remarkable moment this was.

This—not that he had any way to gauge it or prove it—seemed to be one of those moments families have. A mundane moment. An everyday kind of moment.

It made him want to go to a video place and argue about

movie rentals. Or what to have for dinner. Or where to go on vacation.

It felt so damn good he wanted to laugh. He wanted to haul these two girls into his arms and never let them go.

"Here," Savannah said. "Absolutely."

"Good?" Matt asked, arching his eyebrows at Katie.

"Yeah!" she said and Matt lifted the fountain out of the way so they could start digging the hole. He found the pipe extensions he needed and within a few hours they had a working fountain.

"Come on," Katie whined, "show it to us."

"Nope." Matt patted the damp burlap. "I want it to be a surprise."

Katie looked mulish and Savannah bumped her with her hip. "Won't it be cool when he shows us everything tomorrow?" she asked. "When all the flowers are planted and the fountain is going, won't that be the best?"

Katie shrugged.

"What's wrong?" Matt asked, thinking maybe he should relent on the whole unveiling thing. The kid had had a pretty rough couple of days. Maybe she could help plant or something.

"The best would be if you didn't leave," Katie said, blowing a hole right through his chest. He put his hand against the fountain as the earth wobbled slightly.

"Katie," Savannah breathed. "Don't—"

"Why do you have to go?" Katie asked, talking over her mother. "Why can't you just stay?"

"He lives in St. Louis, honey," Savannah said, looking tight and drawn. Paper-thin.

There was something in the air, something hot and worried. She was running blind, he could see it. And he wondered whether she was doing it so she wouldn't get hurt, or to stop him from thinking he should stay.

He'd never know unless he acted.

This was his moment. Right here. Now.

"Savannah?" he said, reaching for her hand but she twisted away.

"What?" She turned to him, her eyes wild. He realized how scared she was, but he wasn't sure what she was so scared of. "You can't stay, can you?"

It was more of an accusation than a question.

"No," he said and Savannah's lips went white, her shoulders going rigid and tight as if taking a punch.

"See?" Her voice broke slightly as she turned to Katie. "He—"

"But I can come back," he said, gripping her hand, turning her to face him, forcing her to look into his eyes. She was blank, carefully blank, as if showing some kind of emotion, some kind of fear or hope, would bring her to her knees. Suddenly, he was desperate to convince her, to shake off that terrible stillness so he could see something true. So he could see the real Savannah.

"I have a couple months' work to finish up in St. Louis," he continued. "But then, I can come back. I..." He glanced at Katie, who was staring at them slack-jawed. "I want to come back."

Savannah's face was still unreadable, but he felt her hands shake as she pulled them out of his, small tremors, cracks throughout her foundation. "We don't have to talk about this right now."

"Why not?"

Finally, something in her flashed, her eyes got hot. "Because we've known each other three weeks, Matt, and half that time you were lying to me. The other half you were killing yourself in my courtyard with guilt over the Elements accident and now, suddenly, you're over it and ready to move here?"

That pissed him off, summing up the relationship that way so she could dismiss it.

"I'm not a child, Savannah. I know how I feel."

"Really?" she asked, laughing slightly and her scorn stung, like nails across his skin. "I find that hard to believe."

He stepped close. Her heat had lit his own fuse and he was suddenly pissed off that she doubted him.

"Are you so ready to throw away what we've got?" he asked.

"And what exactly do we have?"

His eyes narrowed, his muscles tightened. "Don't try to pretend you don't feel something, Savannah. You don't let people close to you, I know that. And yet—" he spread his arms, painfully aware of his eight-year-old audience "—here I am."

Her eyelids flinched. "I don't understand why you're so ready to throw away your life for a woman you've known less than a month."

"I don't think of it as throwing away my life. I can be an architect anywhere," he said, "and St. Louis is no longer my home."

"And the Manor is?" she asked, her eyes wide. "It's that easy for you?"

"I'm not saying this is my home," he snapped. "And I'm not saying that we should get married tomorrow. But I feel something here. Something real and—"

Savannah stepped away as if from a fire that was flaring out of control. "This isn't the time or place," she said, every wall, every defense and barrier in place. She was impenetrable. Unknowable.

Katie stood behind her, owl-eyed and Matt realized Savannah was right. They could talk later.

But, come hell or high water, they would talk.

SAVANNAH, THE COWARD didn't come down for dinner. She didn't come to play cards. Matt played Rachmaninoff again, pounding out the chords, throwing all of his anger into the stormy movements, trying to call her downstairs. Trying desperately to compel her to him.

She didn't show.

But he could feel her upstairs in her room. A room, in all his sneaking around, he'd never gotten into and now, suddenly, it felt like a mystery. As if there were things hidden there that were far more important than jewels.

He imagined her bedroom, clean and uncluttered. Polished and lovely. Understated, like her.

And he wanted so badly to be in both of them.

"Matt," Margot said, standing in the doorway. "Not that the music isn't beautiful, but it's a little…stirring for the middle of the night."

He jerked his hands off the keys feeling wasted. Tomorrow could very well be his last day here and he couldn't believe Savannah wasn't going to talk to him.

"Go upstairs and get her," Margot said.

"That easy, huh?" he asked, not believing it for a second.

"No." Margot laughed. "Not that easy at all. Nothing about Savannah is, but it's what makes her love all the better."

"I know that," he said. "I just don't know how to convince her."

Margot stepped into the room and sat in the wing chair, the moonlight pooling in her lap. "When she first came here, after her mother dropped her off," Margot said, "she was like one of those cats you bring home from the humane society. She hid for about two weeks. For a few days I left out food. Then, once I discovered where she was hiding—in the closet behind all the coats—I opened the door and sat outside in the hall. I didn't say anything, I just sat there and read. Day after day, trying to let her know that I was here. That I was always going to be here."

"What happened?" Matt whispered, feeling his heart break for that girl.

"One night, I felt a cold little body curled up next to mine in my bed."

Matt took a deep ragged breath.

"She's been left a lot," Margot said. "Her mother, her brothers, Katie's father."

"I want to come back," he said, defensively. "I want to be with her, but there are—"

Margot held up her hand. "I understand that," she said. "You need to make *her* understand that."

Matt stood. "I love her," he said.

"That's a start," Margot answered and Matt took off for the stairs and Savannah's room.

SAVANNAH WAS STARING at the ceiling.

She was one of those stupid women in movies after all, wasting so much time ceiling gazing. Ridiculous.

The only problem was she couldn't seem to stop. Her body was so heavy, her head so full of Matt, there wasn't room for anything else. All of her energy was concentrated on keeping a grip on her heart.

Suddenly, the door to her room pushed open and she sat up to find Matt, stormy and dark, in her doorway. His green eyes widened as he took in the room, the pillows and lace, the giant four-poster bed and the canopy.

"What are you doing here?" she snapped, pitching herself off the bed.

"I'm here for that talk," he said, stepping inside, all long-legged grace and masculine energy. God, he was so attractive her body hurt with wanting him. "You know—"

he touched the edge of the canopy "—when I first got here I made a map of the house and I inspected every room looking for any clue of the gems."

"And?"

"I never got in here." His gaze leveled her. "You keep it locked."

"That's not a crime."

"I thought you were hiding the gems."

She laughed, on edge and nervous simply from his being here.

"But you're hiding yourself, aren't you? All this lace, these silly little details. It's all you."

"Architect, gardener and now psychologist?"

"Every night for the past four nights we've slept in the sleeping porch and you were going to let me leave tomorrow without ever showing me this."

"My bed?" she asked, laughing because he was so right. He saw right through her and that grip she had on her heart was slipping. "Here it is." She shifted sideways and flung out her arms. "I asked for a princess bed on the first Christmas I spent with Margot and she got me this monster, the most elaborate princess bed known to man."

She crossed her arms over her chest. "Satisfied?"

His eyes flared and her body got hot. Damp.

"You should go," she said, wishing her voice was stronger. "You're leaving tomorrow—I really don't understand why you want to draw this out."

His body crowded hers, his chest touched her crossed arms and she had to turn her head or drown in his scent. God, she wished he'd just go. Just leave so she could—

"I love you," he said.

And her heart slipped right out of her hands, shattering into a million little pieces.

"Savannah?" he said, tilting her face up, forcing her

to look at him. She couldn't bear it—he was the brightest thing she'd ever seen and looking at him blinded her. Ruined her.

"I have to go," he said, pressing a kiss to her neck. "I have to fix some things I've let fall apart in the last six months. I've made promises—"

"I know." She gasped, his breath making all the hair on her body stand up.

"But I will be back," he said.

"Don't." She put her hand over his lips, so close to totally falling apart she couldn't stand it. "Don't make promises you might not be able to keep."

He shook his head, his eyes hot. "I am not your mother," he said, his voice shot with fire. "And I am neither of your brothers and I am sure as hell not Eric." His hands gripped her arms. "Did you hear me? I love you. *You.*" He flung out his hand, indicating the lace and the bed. "I love this ridiculous room. I love you as the prison warden and the ice princess and the sexy librarian. I love you as a mother and a granddaughter. I love you for your perfect skin and beautiful face and your body that makes me crazy." His hands cupped her head, his fingers pulling the fine hairs at the nape of her neck, the pain so sweet. "I love you for your giant brain."

God, hope was so painful. It was as though her flesh was ice and it was breaking, cold and sharp.

"I love you for your daughter and all your contradictions and complications. But, most of all I love you for your fierce heart."

She closed her eyes, overcome. Every gate had been stormed, every defense in ruins.

He started to pull at her clothes, unzipping zippers, undoing buttons and she let him. She would take his body, his sex and his love, she'd take it all because she really didn't believe that once he left he'd ever cross her threshold again. She would hoard those memories for all the lonely days ahead. "I want that fierce heart to love me back," he said.

It does, she thought but wasn't foolish enough to say it.

"And I know," he continued, kissing her collarbone as he undid her bra, her breasts spilling into his hands. "I know that you love me and I'll be back so you can say it to me."

She pressed her lips to his, sealing her mouth, preventing herself from saying all the things she shouldn't.

HOURS LATER, the kitchen was dark and hushed as they sat side by side on the counter, sweat cooling on their bruised and sated bodies.

Matt had no clue what she was thinking. What was happening behind that still and lovely face.

He took another bite of his ham sandwich and wondered why love had to be so hard, why he felt the pull of her body and the push of her heart and why it all had to hurt so much.

His soul lay between them, a naked offering cold and shivering in all this silence.

"Okay," she said, holding her uneaten sandwich in her lap. She picked at the crust.

"Okay, what?"

Her eyes were damp, tears and moonlight pooling in the corners. Her smile was shaky and nervous, but still the most beautiful smile he'd ever seen. "Come back to me."

It wasn't love, but it was trust, and maybe that was better. From a woman like Savannah, maybe that was the key to her kingdom.

"Savannah," he whispered, joy pumping into his body like fuel. "You have—"

The violent shattering of glass destroyed the quiet of the night.

CHAPTER SEVENTEEN

MATT LEAPED OFF THE counter as though it was on fire. Savannah was right beside him, her hand a talon on his arm.

"What—"

"The sleeping porch," Matt said, turning toward where the crash had come from, adrenaline hammering his system. "Stay here."

"Like hell," she muttered and followed him down the dark hallway to the gloomy half-light of the sleeping porch. "So help me," she whispered, "if it's Garrett or Owen—"

A small figure, dressed in black from head to toe, crossed the doorway of the sleeping porch, between them and the moonlight.

A ski mask. A flashlight no bigger than a pin.

This was no high-schooler.

He felt the sudden blast of fear roll off of Savannah.

Matt shoved his hand out, pressing her against the wall. She nodded when he looked at her. She'd be quiet. She'd be still.

His fingers traced her cheek for a split second, then he snuck through the shadows of the hallway and stepped into the sleeping porch. The thief was short and thin like a kid—maybe it was a teenager after all. One who'd seen a few too many movies about thieves and knew the costume requirements.

He grabbed the kid's arm, hauling him close and the kid turned. Matt got the impression of narrowed blue eyes just before the kid hoofed him—hard—right in the crotch.

Matt gasped and hit the floor.

"Savannah." He tried to gasp in warning, but the thief leaped over him toward the door before he could get out the breath, much less the words.

Forcing himself to swallow the nausea and crushing pain in his groin, he crawled toward the door, pulling himself to his feet in time to see Savannah tackle the thief to the hardwood floor of the hallway.

The thief fought, but Savannah ducked her head to keep her nose and eyes safe and held on tight, her whole body taut with effort.

Fierce wasn't the half of it.

"Good catch," Matt said, hauling the thief off Savannah. He wrapped his arm around the kid's neck to keep him in place then yanked off the ski mask.

Long blond hair fell out around a beautiful and terribly familiar face.

"Mom?" Savannah breathed.

SAVANNAH FELL BACK against the wall, her legs nonexistent. Her whole body eviscerated. She'd stepped down some rabbit hole or something, because looking at her mother was like looking into a mirror. Or into the past. She was unchanged. Her mother stood there, as lovely as the day she left.

As lovely and as cold.

How could this be happening?

Savannah had to shut her eyes and pretend this was a dream. Or that she'd finally lost her mind because there was no way, no way in hell, her mother was back.

And breaking into my home?

Yeah, I hit my head or something. This can't be happening.

"Hello, Savannah," Vanessa said. And the voice was real, carved right out of Savannah's memories. The voice that had read her bedtime stories when she was little. The voice that had sung her songs and scolded her brothers for picking on her.

The voice that had said goodbye and lied.

This was real. This was now.

Rage, bitter and hot, a thousand times stronger than grief, pounded through her.

"Get out of here," Savannah snapped.

"Whoa!" Matt cried. "Wait a second, let's get some answers here. Your mother just broke into your house."

Savannah looked at Matt. She saw the nobility of him and all that love he had for her and wanted to howl. That love was a dream, an illusion.

Her mother was real, standing here after a twenty-year absence.

"She's not my mother," Savannah said, nasty and cold. "She's no one."

"I'm your daughter's grandmother," Vanessa said, such a vicious low blow that Savannah jerked into action, stepping right into her mother's face.

"You stay away from Katie," she hissed. Then understanding dawned. "That was you?" she whispered. "That second break-in through Katie's room?"

"I didn't even know you had a daughter," Vanessa said, her eyes suddenly full. "I'm a grandmother and I didn't know. She's so beautiful, Savvy. So—"

Savannah reeled back. What was this? Grief? Regret? A thousand strings attached to her stomach yanked and she thought she might be sick.

"You left me," she stammered. "You walked away. Twenty years ago! You don't get to cry. You don't get—"

"I missed you," Vanessa said. "Every minute of all of those years, I missed you."

Savannah put her hand to her head, a sudden headache. A sudden desire to scream clawing its way up her throat.

"Then you probably shouldn't have left," Matt said. "You probably shouldn't have abandoned your children."

"What the hell do you know about it?" Vanessa said, pushing at him, a little snarl replacing those tears.

"I know you don't leave behind your kids," Matt said, pushing back. "And then break into their home and make them feel unsafe."

"I'm not here to hurt anyone," Vanessa said, her eyes pleading in Savannah's direction and Savannah wanted to burn down the building with everything she felt. Fires raged inside of her, questions and anger and hurt. Every single thing she thought she'd gotten over was right here as she stared into her mother's lovely face.

Why did you leave me?

What is wrong with me?

Why does everyone go?

"Savannah," Vanessa said. "You have to listen to me. There is a fortune in gems hidden in this house. We could find them. You and I. We could—"

"Where have you been?" Savannah interrupted. "All these years?"

Vanessa's eyes grew colder, harder, the charade of the loving absentee mother falling apart. "Here and there," Vanessa said, rushing on to add, "But I was always thinking of you. I tried to come back, I tried—"

Savannah felt hollow. Lies. All she'd get from her own mother were lies.

"Why are you here now?" Matt asked.

"I don't think that's any of your business," Vanessa answered.

"My father is Joel Woods," he said and Vanessa's eyes flared, her face growing older, uglier every minute.

"Did you steal those gems from Joel and hide them here?" Savannah asked

Vanessa jaw clenched. "No—"

"You're lying."

"I swear—"

"Get out!" Savannah yelled. "Get out of here. That man is in jail and he's twice the person you are. He stayed with his son. Taught him how to play cards and music. Made him macaroni and cheese when he was hungry. What did you do, Mom? Twenty years I waited for you!"

"I swear to you, Savannah. I didn't steal those gems."

"I can't believe a word you say."

"Fine. Maybe we should wake Margot up and ask her if she knows about the gems," Vanessa said.

"I'm already awake," Margot said, in the doorway, cinching the belt on her robe. "And I've called the police."

Vanessa jerked at that, but Matt held on tight.

"I told you, you weren't welcome in my home," Margot said. "Twenty years ago I said if you left these children here, you weren't to come back."

"They're my kids!" Vanessa cried.

"Stop pretending you're here for me!" Savannah yelled. "Stop pretending you care. If you cared, you'd have never left."

"I had things I had to do, honey," Vanessa said, looking like every con man that ever was.

As suddenly as it arrived, the rage left Savannah, taking all of her strength, leaving her weak and sad and small. There was no point to this. None at all.

"Matt," Savannah sighed. "Can you throw her out of my house?"

"Ask her about the gems, Savvy," Vanessa cried. "Ask Margot about Richard—"

"Richard?" Savannah asked and Matt cleared his throat.

"My father's partner was Richard Bonavie," he said quietly.

"My dad?" Savannah cried. "My dad was involved in this and you're just telling me now?"

Matt's eyes flickered to Margot and Savannah spun to face her grandmother. "You *knew?*" she whispered.

"I didn't think it was relevant," Margot said.

Savannah's head nearly exploded.

"You see, Savannah?" Vanessa whispered. "You see how she manipulates? How she lies and turns everything around? Ask her about the gems." Vanessa laughed. "Better yet, ask your dear grandmother why I never came back. Really. Ask her about the money."

"Money?" Savannah whispered.

"Ten thousand dollars a year to stay away from my own kids."

Savannah turned to her grandmother.

"She would have been back every year," Margot said, fierce, like a too-bright light and Savannah hurt looking at her. "She'd be back and play house with you children. She'd toy with you and then vanish again. It's what she'd done her whole life. She wasn't about to change."

"You didn't give me a chance," Vanessa said.

Savannah stared at her grandmother, those familiar eyes. That face she loved so much.

"I did what I thought was best," Margot said. "And I'd do it again."

Savannah felt the walls pressing in on her. A thousand

pounds on her head, stopping her heart. She could barely breathe. It was impossible to think.

Everyone had betrayed her. Everyone.

"Now," Vanessa said, "let's ask her about where she's hidden the gems."

"Do you know anything about the gems?" Savannah asked, so weary, so tired she could barely stand.

"Are you honestly going to believe her?" Margot asked.

"And you're so trustworthy?" she asked. Margot swallowed, shrinking a little and looking more and more her age, which heaped more pain on Savannah's shoulders.

"I'm so sorry, Savannah," Margot whispered. "I have always done what I thought was best."

"So, no gems?" Savannah asked and Margot shook her head.

"She's lying!" Vanessa cried. "Again! Savannah, listen to me, baby—"

"Matt," Savannah whispered, "please get my…mother out of here."

"Out of your house?" he asked. "She broke in looking for those gems. She knows something about the night my father—"

He stopped, blinked. And he grew, right in front of her. Changed. His shoulders suddenly seemed wider, his back straighter and his love for her practically blazed out of his eyes.

She realized what he was doing—curbing his want, his desire for information. He was putting himself on hold, this single-minded man who put his vision aside for no one.

He was putting it aside for her.

She wanted to believe in it, but couldn't. Couldn't find the faith.

Don't, she wanted to say. *I can't repay that. I can't match that sacrifice. I have nothing to give you.*

"You want her gone, she's gone," he said.

"Thank you," she whispered, unable to turn down what he offered so easily when she knew she should.

"Those gems are here, Savannah!" Vanessa yelled as Matt led her out to the front lawn where the cops would soon arrive. "Margot knows something!"

Margot spread her fingers across her belly as if she had a pain. "That woman would have ruined your life."

"Ruined?" A bubble of hysteria built in Savannah. "And how would that be any different than it is now."

"I love you," Margot said. "Every day I've loved you more. You're the daughter—" Margot stopped, tears flooding her eyes, her voice thick. "You're my daughter."

Savannah thought about Matt and his father—those weeks of macaroni and cheese and the forgiveness that Matt gave him. Maybe tomorrow she'd find that forgiveness, somewhere. Somehow. But right now she was empty. Nothing but echoes and hurt.

Savannah stepped past Margot without a word.

She climbed up the stairs to her daughter's room and pressed her hand to the door as if she could feel Katie through the wood. And she could. In her mind she could feel her daughter anywhere.

There was no doubt in her mind that her own mother had never felt that connection. Not once.

But Margot did. Savannah knew, because she felt the same connection to Margot.

Savannah braced her head against the door, exhausted and sore.

The door slid open soundlessly and she crept in, easing herself into Katie's bed, curling her body around Katie's body, her own tiny heart.

MATT GAVE HIS STATEMENT to the cops and watched them put Vanessa, snarling like a rabid dog, into the back of a cruiser.

"Thanks, Matt," Juliette said, stepping beside him so the car could leave. "Tell Savannah I'll be by tomorrow morning."

Matt nodded and waited for her to drive away, then he nearly ran to the house, desperate to stop what he saw in Savannah's eyes.

It was like watching a person bleeding out right in front of you and not being able to stop it. Every second he spent away from her he knew he was losing her. He knew it. He saw it.

He needed to get to her, to get close, to show her that he was here. That no matter where he went—St. Louis, the North Pole, the moon, he was here for her. His heart was right beside hers. If she'd let him in.

The sleeping porch was empty. The kitchen dark. The light was on under Margot's door, but he doubted Savannah was there.

His compass told him she was upstairs. Instead of going to her room he went to Katie's—somehow sensing her need to be close to her baby.

He knocked softly on the door and after a few moments it cracked open, revealing Savannah and her haunted empty eyes.

Speechless in front of all that pain, he reached for her fingers where they curled against the door. One touch and she shifted away, her fingers twitching.

Worry crowded his throat.

"Are you okay?" he asked, hating the stupidity of that question but not knowing where else to start.

She blinked and licked her lips. "Sure," she lied.

"Savannah. You don't have to pretend—"

"I'm tired," she whispered and glanced behind her. "And I don't want to wake up Katie."

"Okay." He wondered how he could even see her, she was so far away.

He waited until she shut the door in his face before hanging his head and retreating to the sleeping porch.

CHAPTER EIGHTEEN

"IT's STUNNING," Margot said the next afternoon, her face radiant with a bright smile. Matt felt an insane amount of pride. He was overwhelmed with it, actually. Humbled by it. "It's so..."

"Totally perfect!" Katie cried, spinning around in a circle, taking in what, Matt had to admit, was a totally perfect courtyard.

The flowers were planted, small hills and valleys of pinks and greens. Roses and hostas. Forget-me-nots, bougainvillaea and birds of paradise. Wisteria, lilac, honeysuckle. It was fragrant to the extreme, and he would never smell another flower without thinking of these women.

The cypress was trimmed and magnificent, the cobblestones replaced by a stunning carpet of green. The wall, barely visible in the back, was strong and would stay that way for a hundred years. The new greenhouse, a kit he'd ordered and modified, gleamed in the late afternoon sunlight.

This was his gift, his offering, his heart, beating and red with blood—for Savannah.

Savannah, who was silent. She stood to the side, her arms across her chest. She looked so thin, so small. Lost in the icy distance between her and everyone else.

How do I get to her, he wondered, panicked. *How do I reach her?*

"What do you think?" he asked Savannah.

"It's so beautiful, Matt," Savannah whispered. "It's…" She smiled slightly and his heart chugged. "I'm speechless."

"What about the fountain?" Katie asked, pointing to the burlap-covered structure in the seedling maze.

"Let's check it out," he said, leading the way, his troop of women fanning out behind him. When they were all standing around the fountain he'd had a friend ship to him—a piece he'd long admired for a long time but had no place for—he untied the twine and pulled off the rough brown cover.

Three delicate copper-and-steel women danced in a circle, long hair streaming, arms raised in jubilation, their mouths open wide as if singing or laughing. Red and pink enamel flowers laced their hair and filled their hands. Blue birds and yellow butterflies darted amongst them.

When he turned on the valve, the fountain spun and the women danced in a light rain.

The girls were silent. Matt could hear them breathing.

"Is that us?" Katie asked.

He nodded. "Those are my wild and unpredictable O'Neill women." He palmed Katie's head, giving it a shake.

In the silence the fountain spun and Matt's heart pounded.

"I remember when you were born, Savannah, honey," Margot said, her voice choked with tears, her gaze on Savannah like a spotlight. "Carter and Tyler were born up north, but Vanessa came home when she was pregnant with you. She was so big, I thought you were going to weigh ten pounds." Margot laughed and sniffed, digging in her pocket for a tissue. "There was something going on with her. She said that she and Richard were having a fight, but I knew it was something more. Something bad she was running from. Carter—" she blew out a big breath "—Carter was like a guard dog over Tyler, it made me so scared something had happened to one of them. With the company Vanessa kept, it only seemed a matter of time before someone got it in their head to hurt one of the little boys." She shook her head, her lips pressed tight as if keeping the worst of her fears locked inside. "Anyway, Vanessa went into labor in the middle of the night. Real fast. Asleep one minute, screaming her head off the next. We got her into the hospital in the nick of time—I swear I thought you were going to be born into my arms on the front lawn."

Katie laughed and even Savannah had to smile. Matt's heart was breaking.

"Vanessa couldn't breast-feed," Margot said. "You wouldn't latch, stubborn little thing. She tried, but you wanted nothing to do with her."

Savannah's face crumpled slightly as if bending under the weight she was trying to hold up.

"So I fed you," Margot said. "So little in my arms— nothing but eyelashes and temper—that was you. I held you in my arms and you blinked open those big blurry eyes and shook your little fists at me. And then you focused. On me. You grabbed my finger. Mine." Margot's voice broke and her trembling hands pressed against her chest. "I loved you so much I could barely stand it, and I promised you that first night, walking the hallways of that hospital with you in my arms, I promised I would do what I had to do to keep you safe."

Matt held his breath, hoping against hope that Savannah could forgive Margot for making the choices she'd made.

"Why didn't you tell me about the money?" Savannah asked.

"I didn't know how," Margot said. "No, that's not true. I didn't want to. I didn't want to explain what I knew about your mother. That this was the only way I could think of to keep you all safe."

"When did you stop?" Savannah asked.

"Stop? I haven't."

"What?" Savannah cried. "You're still paying her?"

Margot's hand twitched. "Katie."

"What's happening?" Katie whispered.

Matt put his hand on the girl's head. "Give them a second."

Savannah blew out a heavy breath. "I can't believe this."

"I figured someday you'd ask." Margot's laugh was coated in tears. "The house is falling apart and I never seem to have any money. I've sold the paintings, the china, almost everything of value. I almost wish I had those gems so I could keep the roof from falling down on our heads."

"I just thought…" Savannah dug her hands into her hair. "I thought you were gambling everything away. I've been saving money thinking I would buy the house if it came to that."

"Oh, honey—"

"I had no idea you were paying my mother to stay away." Savannah flung out her arms. "God, it sounds so ridiculous."

"It is. It's absolutely ridiculous," Margot said. "But it was the best I could do. You're a mother, Savannah. You understand."

Savannah nodded, her smile watery as she stared at the fountain. "I understand. I do. It's just going to take me a while to get my head around it."

Margot's eyes closed in what appeared to be sublime

relief. "Well," she said, her voice lighter, "don't take too long. I'm an old woman."

"Not that old." Savannah touched Margot's hand then squeezed it hard.

Finally, Margot turned her attention to Matt—the high beams of her charm and affection nearly blinding him. "As for you," she said, "you are a miracle. A—" The tears she'd kept controlled until now streamed down her cheeks. "A blessing. I didn't realize how badly we needed you until you showed up on my door."

"It's only a garden," he whispered, touched by her sentiment.

"No, it is not," she said, suddenly a dragon. "It is so much more and you are so much more." Margot wrapped her arms around him, hugged him hard. "Don't give up on her," she whispered. "She needs you now more than ever."

Margot stepped back and took Katie's hand. "Let's go make some celebration lemonade," she said, giving Katie's arm a shake. "And maybe a sugar pie."

Katie leaped away, jumping toward the kitchen and the promise of sugar pie.

Now it was only Matt and Savannah standing in the sun-drenched courtyard, the fountain's whirr and splash joining the mad pounding of his heart.

Matt couldn't look away from Savannah, couldn't stop wishing that she would look at him. He was beginning to get angry with himself, acting like a homeless dog searching for scraps.

He used to be better than this, but Savannah had changed the rules. She'd changed the whole game.

"I'll stay," he blurted and Savannah's gaze flew to his, wide and surprised. "I don't have to go back just yet. I'll call." He dug into his pocket for his phone but Savannah's cool hand stopped him.

Stopped his heart, to be honest.

"Don't, Matt. You have to go back, you've made promises. And if you broke those now you'd never forgive yourself."

"A few days, a few—"

"No, Matt."

"Do you want me to leave?" he asked, shaken to the core.

"No!" she cried. "No, I don't want you to leave, but I understand that you have to."

"I'm so sorry," he whispered, relieved. "I'm sorry that I have to leave, that your mother showed up the way that she did, that Margot…" There was so much on her shoulders. So much pain. So much betrayal. "I don't know how to make this right for you."

"It's not up to you to make this right," she said. "It doesn't actually have anything to do with you."

Her words were a wrecking ball and anger slammed through him. "How can you say that?" he asked. "I love you. Everything that hurts you hurts me."

She stared at him, her eyes wide as though she didn't get it. Something awful was beginning to build inside of him. Not just doubt or anger, but something dark and big and worse than the building collapse. Like a poison, black and thick, reality crested.

"Do you love me, Savannah?"

She didn't say anything for a long time then, as though it was a secret or something to be ashamed of, she whispered, "Yes."

And he didn't even feel joy over her admission, because he knew, looking at her, that she wished she didn't love him.

"God, listen to you," he said, wanting to laugh. Wanting, actually, to scream. "The only person on the planet who thinks love is bad."

"It's not bad," she said. "It hurts. I know you don't think you'll hurt me, but you will. It's what people do. It's unavoidable."

"Do you believe me when I say that I'll be back?"

Savannah licked her lips, her shoulders straight. "I believe that right now you mean it."

"I don't know how to convince you," he said. "What can I do?"

Savannah blinked and blinked again, silent and damning. She would never believe him. She would never be convinced of his love.

Suddenly it dawned on him, what the rest of his life would be like if he returned to her.

"Every day would be a test," he said. "I could come back, move in. Start my life over with you. But it wouldn't be enough, because every day you'd be expecting me to walk out. Every day I would have to prove myself to you."

She looked down at her hands, and a big fat tear splotched across her knuckle. "Please come back," she said. "Please. I will try, I really will. I will try to trust—"

He was overwhelmed by an anger and a heartache so big he almost collapsed under its weight. "No, Savannah," he whispered. "I won't. I can't."

Her eyes, blue and wounded, flew to his. "Wh-what?"

"I can't give you faith," he said. "I can't make you have it, or force you to feel it. You've got to do that part on your own, Savannah. If you love me, really love me and want to spend your life with me the way I want to spend my life with you, you have to have faith in me. In you. Us. You have to come to me, otherwise we're doomed."

His hands fumbled as he pulled out his wallet, his fingers shook as he dug out a card. He took her hand, memorizing the fine long fingers, the calluses across her palm that she'd gotten working alongside him. He pressed the card into her palm then dropped her hand. Another minute and he wouldn't go. Another second and he'd do this her way and they'd never have a chance.

"I'll be waiting, Savannah," he whispered.

And before he lost the strength to walk away, he left. He left his bag. His clothes. His heart. Everything.

He had his wallet, the keys to his car and the clothes on his back.

I'll never see her again, he thought and wanted to die.

It was the last day of summer school and Savannah watched from her post at the returns desk as Owen's former girlfriend, The Cheerleader, got cozy under Garrett's arm.

Garrett had a black eye that was fading to yellow and Owen had made friends with some new hoodlums on the other side of the computer bank. New hoodlums who were eyeing Savannah over their screens.

"I heard he killed a guy," one of them whispered. "It was an accident, but still."

"He's like some hotshot architect or something. He was just pretending to be a gardener."

"Shut up." Garrett sneered. "Like Ms. O'Neill's got a boyfriend. Give me a break."

Shut up indeed, she thought, trying hard to block out the whispers as well as any thought of Matt. It was like a small electric shock every time she allowed a memory of his touch, or his laugh, or the look in those green eyes when he said he wouldn't be back, to flicker through her head.

She was tired, so tired of resisting the pain.

Particularly when it all hurt anyway.

"Don't you listen to what they say," Janice whispered, bringing a pile of books from the oak tables to the desk for reshelving. "They're a bunch of foul-mouthed jerks."

"It's true," Savannah said in a clear speaking voice that sounded like machine-gun fire in the hushed atmosphere of the library.

Janice dropped the books.

"All of it." Savannah kept talking, driven by some need to protect Matt from the fate she was drowning in. Her eyes met the astonished eyes of the high school kids. "Every single thing you've ever whispered about me, totally true."

"Savannah." Janice tugged on her arm. "Maybe lower your voice."

"No!" Savannah said and the echo was so nice. So loud and hard and cold.

"You're having some kind of psychotic break," Janice said and Savannah laughed, the sound rolling and rolling and rolling through the library, filling the corners with its hysteria.

"Probably," she said. "I *am* an O'Neill, after all. I slept with a married man and my mother is a thief and liar. My brother is a gambler and my grandmother—" she turned to Janice "—what would you call my grandmother?"

"A very nice lady—"

"A whore." Savannah nodded as if they were all in agreement. "You'd call her a whore. And all of us, every single one of the Notorious O'Neills, is alone. We live alone and we die alone."

"I'm calling Margot," Janice said and disappeared.

"But Matt Woods didn't murder anyone," Savannah said, advancing on the teenagers who'd been whispering. They backed up, falling out of their chairs, astonished and terrified of Savannah.

Good, she thought, victorious. *Let them all be terrified.* Because what Savannah was feeling these days, this poisonous mix of grief and longing and anger at herself and her world—it was terrifying.

I let him go, the thought her constant companion. *I let him walk away.*

"If Matt Woods is too good a man for me," she said, "then Matt Woods is far too good a man to be talked about by you."

He's the best man, she wanted to say.

"Honey," Janice said softly, as though Savannah was a mad dog or a suicide threat. "Why don't you come on into your office and have a seat?"

Savannah let herself be led away, but she turned back to the students. "Don't talk about him," she said. "Ever again."

The kids nodded, mouths agape.

Satisfaction was a very dull candle against the blackness of all her grief, but it was something. One small thing.

Missing Matt was like carrying around a thousand extra pounds, and when she sat in her office chair, she collapsed, exhausted.

"Margot's going to come pick you up," Janice said, her chins wobbling, her hands clenched in front of that mountain of bosom.

"I think…" Savannah paused. "I need some time off."

"That stomach thing again?" Janice asked, nodding as though she'd understood all along, and maybe she had.

Who knew what kind of secrets Janice kept with her Fannie May sampler pack.

"I love a man and I let him go," Savannah whispered. "I really love him."

Janice plunked down on the edge of the desk. "Does he love you?" she asked.

Savannah nodded, staring at her hands. Useless, those hands. Numb and unfeeling without Matt to touch.

"Well, honey." Janice sighed. "Men are simple creatures and that's the truth. If they love you, then they're yours. It's just the way it is."

"He wants…too much…too much from me."

"Well," Janice huffed. "Bill tried that, too, in the beginning and I told him that real women aren't like girls in those porno films. We don't—" Janice stopped and turned bright red. "Maybe we're not talking about the same things."

"He wants me to leave Bonne Terre. He wants me to go to him." Even saying it made Savannah's stomach hurt and her head dizzy.

"Well." Janice stood. "That'd be all right. A nice trip— you could take Katie." There was a commotion out by the desk and Janice glanced over her shoulder.

"Well," she said, "everyone's a little wound up out there. I better go take care of things." Janice patted Savannah's shoulder and brushed back the hair she'd been wearing loose for some reason. As though Matt could see it. As though Matt would even know. "You take whatever time you need, Savannah. When Joey was sick last year you were so good to me and I'm happy to return the favor."

Janice was gone and Savannah's office pounded with quiet.

She pressed hands to her head.

It had been four weeks since Matt had left. Four weeks

and three days. The first week she'd kept thinking he would be back. He had to come back. All of his things were in the sleeping porch. Five shirts. Four pairs of pants. The files. His bag. His toothbrush.

But as the first week faded into the second week, she realized he was leaving these things behind the way he'd left her, and the shirts seemed sad. The pants forlorn.

It had only gotten worse. She slept in those shirts. Carried a river stone she'd found in the bottom of his bag in her pocket. She wore his cologne, used the last of his shampoo.

She was losing it. Every day seemed longer and harder to bear. Every night full of misery.

Discovery had more work for her. Not that she cared.

Katie didn't play hide-and-seek anymore. The three of them got together every night and played poker, but it was halfhearted at best.

Matt's chair, still pulled up to the foot of the table as though he'd just gone to the bathroom or gotten a drink, seemed so big. So empty.

The piano collected dust. The house was so silent, so devoid of music it seemed like a black hole.

"Well, look at you," Margot said as she walked into Savannah's office, her hair tied back in a scarf. The ends, blue and green and red, fell over her shoulder. "Giving the gossips something meaty to chew on for a change."

She didn't look her age but no one was going to live forever. Margot would die. And Katie...

"I don't want Katie to live like I do," Savannah said and Margot stepped in, shutting the door behind her. "I don't want her to be scared."

"Of what?" Margot asked as if this conversation made sense.

"Of people, of leaving the Manor, of..." Savannah sighed. "Falling in love."

"Well, then I imagine someone should show her that there's nothing to be afraid of. That falling in love is something to treasure. A gift. A very very rare one."

"Why haven't you been in love?" Savannah asked.

"I was, a very long time ago." Margot sat in the chair across from the desk. "Your grandfather was quite a man. And when he died in Korea, I knew that was it for me. Some people get love like that a few times in their lives, but I wasn't destined to be one of them."

Savannah took a deep breath. "So it's up to me?" she asked. "I've got to show her that love is a gift?"

Margot laughed. "You've got a very good man waiting for you."

"I know," Savannah said. She slipped her hand in her pocket and found that river rock, curled her fingers around it until it seemed to get hot in her palm.

I can do this, she thought. If Matt could put the building collapse behind him and forgive his father and love her enough for the both of them, then she could go to him. She could put her faith in him. In love.

She stood. "I'm going to take Katie on a trip."

"An excellent plan."

"I don't know when I'll be back."

"A very excellent plan."

"I can do this," she said, trying to convince herself.

Margot clasped one of Savannah's hands in both of hers. "You can do anything."

Savannah threw her arms around Margot. "Thank you," she whispered. "Thank you for keeping us safe. Thank you for being the best mother I could have ever wished for."

"You're welcome. Now go get that man before he decides life is easier without you."

Crap. That could really happen? Savannah grabbed her purse and ran out of the library.

The sun was bright and she blinked at its radiance, feeling as if she'd come out of a cave into a brand-new day.

CHAPTER NINETEEN

MATT FLIPPED CARTER'S CARD around in his fingers, the edges of the fine paper getting soft, dingy from wear. To call or not to call, that was the question.

"All right," Erica said, coming into his office with yet another box. "This is the last one." She dropped the heavy box next to the other ten. All that was left of his business. Files he needed to keep. Tax returns. Other documents that seemed too important to shred.

He was getting rid of the office space—the last of the work he could do from home.

"Thank you," he said, pushing back in his chair until it hit the floor-to-ceiling window looking down on Washington Avenue.

"You already have," Erica said, her eyes becoming watery. The Rolex he gave her sparkled tastefully at her wrist, but he knew that wasn't what she was talking about.

"When do classes start?"

"In a few days. Matt—"

He waved his hands. "You're going to be an incredible architect and Washington University will give you the best education."

It had been hard convincing her to take the opportunity, but he knew she'd been saving for the chance to go back to school. He simply sped up the process.

"What are you going to do?" she asked.

"Well, I'm going to finish the Monroes' lake house and the library in Creve Coeur, but then..." He flipped the card again. "We'll see."

"No more disappearing acts?"

He nearly laughed. It seemed like a miracle she could even see him. Every day he woke up and looked in the mirror at his body, and wondered how it was still around. He felt like he was vanishing, bit by bit. A walking, talking ghost.

"I swear," he said and held up his hand. "Now, you should head out before traffic gets too bad."

"Okay," she said. He quickly hugged her, before her tears could start in earnest, and promised to stay in touch, to take care of himself.

Blah, blah, blah.

Matt just wanted to be alone. To lick his wounds. To examine all of his memories of Savannah and Katie in quiet. Torture himself in peace.

She wasn't coming. He knew that. He knew that the second he made the demand. She said she loved him, but without faith, love was shallow. Practically empty.

An hour later he heard the door open again and he spun away from the view he'd been staring at. The sun had set and his office was gray and shadowy, the yellow light from reception cutting a bright slice out of the gloom.

"I told you I'd—"

Savannah stepped into the doorway.

NERVES WERE CUTTING OFF all brain function. Savannah could only look at him and wonder if she was too late.

Do you still want me? she wanted to ask. *Even though I'm a mess? Even though it took me so long to believe in you, in the goodness and wonder of you?*

Her mouth was dry. Her palms damp.

"Hi," she said. *Idiot.*

"Savannah?" He stood, slowly as if in disbelief. He was thin again, pale. But so handsome in a suit, the tie pulled loose.

He wore his glasses. And she just wanted to curl up in his arms and lick him.

"Matt!" Katie barreled into the room, nearly knocking Savannah over in her enthusiasm. "Whoa! Look at that view!" She ran to the window and pressed her face against it, her breath creating condensation against the glass. She'd been this way the whole journey—two days of uncorked curiosity. It was exhilarating. And exhausting. "You're not going to believe it. We saw the Mississippi River. It looks dirty. And we saw a homeless person and we got stuck in traffic. Lots of traffic. We stayed in a motel, Matt. With a pool. Can you believe it?"

"No," he whispered, not taking his eyes off Savannah. "I can't believe it at all."

"I'm…ah…" Savanna lifted her hand, feeling foolish in a hundred different ways. *Sorry?* As if that covered the extent of her emotions. *So in love I can't sleep at night. So in love it hurts being away from you.*

"Here?" he asked, slowly, oh, so slowly circling his big desk.

She nodded, her smile gaining strength. Courage. She gripped the rock in her pocket, her talisman, her compass leading to Matt. "I am. I'm here." Oh, this was the hard part. The killer. "If you still want me?"

"Want you?" he asked, his eyes like flames against the night. He practically stalked her across the room, his look so predatory, and it was thrilling to be the focus of all that desire. All that raw want.

Her body went hot in answer, her heart beat fast in anticipation.

Touch me. Oh, please touch me. I'm so much more real when you touch me. So much more myself.

"I will never stop wanting you," he said. "I love you."

His hand grazed her shoulder and she shuddered in relief, collapsing against him. "I love you, too. Oh, God, I love you."

"I didn't think you'd come," he breathed against her hair.

"Not come?" She looked back at him. "For you?" She brushed aside some of his hair, touched his forehead, his cheeks, the gorgeous beloved curve of his lip. "You can't get away from me now," she said. "I'm unleashed. I'll chase you anywhere."

"This is the only place I want to be," he whispered, pulling her so tight against him she could barely breathe.

And it was perfect.

"Thank you," she whispered. "Thank you for making me do this. Thank you for having faith in me."

"Always," he said. "You are my salvation, Savannah. My light."

"Hey!" Katie cried as he was leaning in to kiss Savannah. "Can we go see that arch thing? And a riverboat, I want to see a riverboat. Mom said we could go see the ocean. Want to come, Matt? Have you seen the ocean?"

"The ocean?" he asked.

"It was a long trip," Savannah said. "And she was so excited. I feel like now that we're away from the Manor we need to see it all. I've taken a leave of absence," she said. "I was hoping..." She looked up at him. "There's a whole world out there, Matt, and I'd like to see some of it. With you."

"And I'd like to show it to you," he whispered. He

kissed her, or she kissed him. She wasn't sure. And it didn't matter.

They were together. And the journey was just beginning.

EPILOGUE

To Carter and Tyler
From Savannah

Hi, guys! I've only got a few minutes before our flight leaves. Matt, Katie and I are on our way to Paris. Matt wants to show me the Eiffel Tower and I want to see it! Katie wants to eat French fries in France—she thinks they'll be better there. She's going to miss some school, but you only live once, right? I know, I can't believe it's me saying that, either.

We're going to be gone for two months and Margot is leaving for another cruise in two weeks so the Manor is going to be empty. Juliette says she can keep an eye on it, but frankly I'm worried. You know Mom broke in a while ago and I didn't press charges. I know what you're thinking, Carter, but I didn't want to take that process on with her. Not when it feels like my whole life is starting.

Anyway, I don't think we've seen the end of her. Carter, I know you're busy being very important and Tyler, you're busy doing...what are you doing, again? But it would mean a lot to me and to Margot if you'd check in on the house. If one of you could keep an eye on things. Carter, I imagine it would be you. Tyler, sorry, but you've never been good at the responsibility thing.

Anyway, I love you both. Life is better than I ever imagined. I'll send postcards.

Love,
Savannah.

* * * * *

Don't miss the continuation of Molly O'Keefe's
THE NOTORIOUS O'NEILLS
miniseries!
Look for the next story
TYLER O'NEILL'S REDEMPTION
Coming in September 2010 from
Harlequin Superromance.

HARLEQUIN *Super Romance*

COMING NEXT MONTH

Available September 14, 2010

LARGER-PRINT BOOKS!
GET 2 FREE LARGER-PRINT NOVELS PLUS
2 FREE GIFTS!

HARLEQUIN®

Super Romance

Exciting, emotional, unexpected!

YES! Please send me 2 FREE LARGER-PRINT Harlequin® Superromance® novels and my 2 FREE gifts (gifts are worth about $10). After receiving them, if I don't wish to receive any more books, I can return the shipping statement marked "cancel." If I don't cancel, I will receive 6 brand-new novels every month and be billed just $5.44 per book in the U.S. or $5.99 per book in Canada. That's a saving of at least 13% off the cover price! It's quite a bargain! Shipping and handling is just 50¢ per book.* I understand that accepting the 2 free books and gifts places me under no obligation to buy anything. I can always return a shipment and cancel at any time. Even if I never buy another book from Harlequin, the two free books and gifts are mine to keep forever.

139/339 HDN E5PS

Name	(PLEASE PRINT)

Address	Apt. #

City	State/Prov.	Zip/Postal Code

Signature (if under 18, a parent or guardian must sign)

Mail to the Harlequin Reader Service:
IN U.S.A.: P.O. Box 1867, Buffalo, NY 14240-1867
IN CANADA: P.O. Box 609, Fort Erie, Ontario L2A 5X3

Not valid for current subscribers to Harlequin Superromance Larger-Print books.

**Are you a current subscriber to Harlequin Superromance books
and want to receive the larger-print edition?
Call 1-800-873-8635 today!**

* Terms and prices subject to change without notice. Prices do not include applicable taxes. N.Y. residents add applicable sales tax. Canadian residents will be charged applicable provincial taxes and GST. Offer not valid in Quebec. This offer is limited to one order per household. All orders subject to approval. Credit or debit balances in a customer's account(s) may be offset by any other outstanding balance owed by or to the customer. Please allow 4 to 6 weeks for delivery. Offer available while quantities last.

Your Privacy: Harlequin Books is committed to protecting your privacy. Our Privacy Policy is available online at www.eHarlequin.com or upon request from the Reader Service. From time to time we make our lists of customers available to reputable third parties who may have a product or service of interest to you. If you would prefer we not share your name and address, please check here. ☐

Help us get it right—We strive for accurate, respectful and relevant communications. To clarify or modify your communication preferences, visit us at www.ReaderService.com/consumerschoice.

HARLEQUIN®

A *Romance*

FOR EVERY MOOD™

Spotlight on
Heart & Home

Heartwarming romances
where love can happen
right when you least expect it.

See the next page to enjoy a sneak peek
from Harlequin Superromance®,
a Heart and Home series.

Enjoy a sneak peek at fan favorite Molly O'Keefe's
Harlequin Superromance miniseries,
THE NOTORIOUS O'NEILLS, *with*
TYLER O'NEILL'S REDEMPTION,
available September 2010
only from Harlequin Superromance.

Police chief Juliette Tremblant recognized the shape of the man strolling down the street—in as calm and leisurely fashion as if it were the middle of the day rather than midnight. She slowed her car, convinced her eyes were playing tricks on her. It had been a long time since Tyler O'Neill had been seen in this town.

As she pulled to a stop at the curb, he turned toward her, and her heart about stopped.

"What the hell are you doing here, Tyler?"

"Well, if it isn't Juliette Tremblant." He made his way over to her, then leaned down so he could look her in the eye. He was close enough to touch.

Juliette was not, repeat, *not* going to touch Tyler O'Neill. Not with her fingers. Not with a ten-foot pole. There would be no touching. Which was too bad, since it was the only way she was ever going to convince herself the man standing in front of her—as rumpled and heart-stoppingly handsome now as he'd been at sixteen—was real.

And not a figment of all her furious revenge dreams.

"What are you doing back in Bonne Terre?" she asked.

"The manor is sitting empty," Tyler said and shrugged, as though his arriving out of the blue after ten years was casual. "Seems like someone should be watching over the family home."

"You?" She laughed at the very notion of him being here for any unselfish reason. "Please."

He stared at her for a second, then smiled. Her heart fluttered against her chest—a small mechanical bird powered by that smile.

"You're right." But that cryptic comment was all he offered.

Juliette bit her lip against the other questions.

Why did you go?

Why didn't you write? Call?

What did I do?

But what would be the point? Ten years of silence were all the answer she really needed.

She had sworn off feeling anything for this man long ago. Yet one look at him and all the old hurt and rage resurfaced as though they'd been waiting for the chance. That made her mad.

She put the car in gear, determined not to waste another minute thinking about Tyler O'Neill. "Have a good night, Tyler," she said, liking all the cool "go screw yourself" she managed to fit into those words.

It seems Juliette has an old score to settle with Tyler.
Pick up TYLER O'NEILL'S REDEMPTION
to see how he makes it up to her.
Available September 2010,
only from Harlequin Superromance.

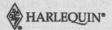

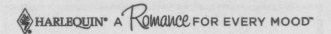